DEATH ON THE
BOARDWALK

Also by Caleb Wygal

Lucas Caine Novels
Moment of Impact
A Murder in Concord
Blackbeard's Lost Treasure
The Search for the Fountain of Youth

DEATH
ON THE
BOARDWALK

A MYRTLE BEACH MYSTERY

CALEB WYGAL

FRANKLIN/KERR
KANNAPOLIS, NORTH CAROLINA

Published by Franklin/Kerr Press
Kannapolis, North Carolina 28083
www.FranklinKerr.com

Edited by S. Daisy
Cover art and design by Mibl Art
Interior design by Jordon Greene

Printed in the United States of America

FIRST EDITION

Hardcover ISBN 978-1-7354373-3-0
Paperback ISBN 978-1-7354373-2-3

Library of Congress Control Number: 2020921605

Fiction: Cozy Mystery
Fiction: Amateur Sleuth
Fiction: Southern Fiction

To my mother-in-law,
Angela DeRemer.
This book would have taken much
longer to write had you not volunteered to
have playtime with the munchkin.
Thank you.

CHAPTER
ONE

There was a rug I wasn't expecting awaiting me in the alcove by the backdoor of my bookstore as I arrived to start the day. The rug had an art deco pattern of periwinkle and sepia toned multi-colored squares with a tan border. Each square was different. Random. It was a nice rug.

Except for the body rolled up in the middle of it.

The rug rested at an angle across the cement slab in a recessed alcove. When I had grasped one end, I felt something odd. A squishy lump. A tremor ran through my hands, jostling the box of pastries I held. Focus. I set the pastries on the ground.

Acid churned in the pit of my stomach. It was too heavy to be a normal rug.

With a trembling hand, I reached down and pulled a corner back.

I immediately knew who it was, despite the deformation that told me the cause of death. A blow to the head. It was obvious. I saw no other marks or injuries to the exposed area of her body.

She was a regular at my bookstore, Myrtle Beach Reads, and a well-known figure in the local business community. We used to sit and have coffee in the store and carry on pleasant conversations about books, life, family, and various causes she involved herself in.

I've read and watched enough murder mysteries to know not to disturb the body. I already had, but I didn't think I had done anything to destroy or disturb evidence. I figured that most of the evidence lay wherever she got bonked on the head.

I returned the corner of the rug to where I found it, covering her face. I rested a hand on the concrete wall to steady myself. Breathed in. Breathed out.

I poked my head out from the delivery alcove and looked both ways down Flagg Street. In one direction, a woman emerged from a parking garage, head intent on her phone, and crossed the street to the Budget Inn. A golf cart receded in the distance past her. Looking to the south, I saw a golf cart cruising in the opposite direction. A beer truck pulled to a stop behind a bar.

I checked my watch. 7:53. Karen wasn't due in for another hour.

My first call was to the police. The phone shook in my hand as I dialed 911. I told the dispatcher what I found, and she instructed me to stay there, but not to touch anything. I told her I had no plans of examining the body and hung up the phone. Then, I called Karen and asked if she could come in early. She answered halfway through the second ring and said she'd be in as soon as she could. I didn't tell her why I needed her.

A salty breeze blew across my skin. I don't know if the wind or the dead body caused me to shiver. A siren wailed in the distance. Both the police station and fire department were about half a mile away. It wouldn't take them long to get here. Especially at this time of day when many tourists were still asleep in their hotels.

The rug was half-rolled over Paige's body. I tried not to look but couldn't help it. A smear of blood matted her blonde hair. I cringed. I didn't like to watch when getting my blood drawn at the doctor's office. I wasn't a fan of horror or bloody movies and books. Besides that, her body and most of the inside of the rug appeared clean. Sections of the outside, or what would be the underside had the rug been unfurled, were filthy and streaked with what looked like grease.

I tried to imagine a scene where she might have been killed. It looked like someone whacked her right on top of the head. She fell over. Thump. Maybe onto this rug, or the killer carried her to it before rolling her up like a burrito. I pictured it covering the floor of an office. Her office, perhaps.

Then what caused the underside to be so filthy?

The question evaporated from my mind as an MBPD cruiser with its lights flashing stopped at the bottom of the two stairs leading down to the ground. A MBFD Fire/Rescue ambulance pulled up a moment later.

A male officer and a female officer saw me standing there and didn't tell me to freeze and put my arms in the air when they exited their vehicle. Whew. The woman got out of the passenger side. She rested a hand on her gun as they surveyed the scene.

"Hello," the guy cop said, raising a dark pair of sunglasses.

"Good morning," I said. Not like there was a dead body at my feet or anything. I almost asked what brought them this way so early but decided against it.

"I'm Officer O'Brien," the driver said and then pointed at his partner. "That's Officer Nichols."

Nichols nodded but did not speak, her hand still resting on the gun. A trickle of sweat ran down my back, despite the cool air. I had no reason to be nervous. I did nothing wrong, but to think they thought me a suspect didn't sit well with me. They likely only knew the scant details I gave to the 911 operator. Which was: a guy found a body rolled up in a rug on Flagg Street between 4th and 5th Avenues.

"Please step aside," O'Brien said.

"Sure thing, officer," I said and did as he instructed.

I've seen both of them around before, though I don't recall ever meeting either. If I recognized them, I'm sure they recognized me. I tend to stick out.

I stepped off the alcove towards them to get out of their path. It was a little tight with the front bumper of the patrol car parked within inches of the building.

Two firefighters leapt from their truck, grabbed some equipment, and rushed to Paige. They ignored me and focused on her.

Nichols finally took her hand off the gun. O'Brien stuck out a thick hand. I shook it. He had a strong grip I tried to match. He and his partner were in good shape under their bulletproof vests. I'd put on a few pounds over the summer and looked flabby compared to them. Too many visits to the Boardwalk Creamery will do that to you. I couldn't help it. I walked past their back door every day. The baking waffle cones to me were like the Sirens to Odysseus.

Nichols turned for a closer look at the body while O'Brien barely glanced at it. He expelled a breath and glanced up at the Myrtle Beach Reads sign above our heads. "You know, I can't remember going in there before."

"Read many books?" I asked.

"Nah, not really. Just police manuals and such."

"You should expand your horizons. I could recommend a good book or two to you sometime."

"I don't know about that. Between three boys, two dogs, and a wife, I don't get much free time."

"Do you like coffee?"

That brought a brief smile. "Of course."

I hooked a thumb at the building. "Got that too."

"Is it good?"

"I like to think so. I only brew locally roasted beans made within the last week."

His bottom lip puckered out. "I'll have to stop in sometime."

"Do that. First cup is on me. Probably not today, though."

"Not likely," he squinted. He pulled out a paper tablet, flipped a page, and clicked a ballpoint pen. "Tell me what happened."

"There's not much to tell. I parked my Jeep back on Chester Street like I always do, grabbed my pastries," I pointed at the box from Benjamin's Bakery on the ground beside me, "and came around the corner. I said a few words to Theresa—"

"Who is she?"

"She owns the I Heart MB Tees place two doors down."

He made a note. "Did she act or seem like anything was amiss?"

"Not that I could tell."

"Okay. Continue."

A rustling sound came from behind me. I turned to see one of the firefighters moving one corner of the rug away from the body. I quickly twisted back to O'Brien and Nichols. I'd already seen more than I wanted to.

He put a calming hand on my shoulder. "It's okay, man. We'll take care of her. I'm sorry you have to experience this, but your help here could lead us to finding who did this."

By now, people started to gather around. Not too close, but far enough away that they could see that something was happening without being a part of it. The sight of a police car parked this time of the morning in this area was a rare occurrence. I saw a few familiar faces, and I knew that I'd be the talk of the Boardwalk, at least for today.

I drew a breath.

"There's not much more to it," I said. "I saw the rug as the recess came into view. I hadn't ordered one, so I knew it shouldn't have been there. I saw it was misshapen as I got closer."

"What do you mean by misshapen?"

"It didn't look right. It was fatter than a rolled rug, and it was lumpy."

O'Brien scrawled a few notes. "Go on."

"As I stepped up to it, I had a bad feeling. I unrolled it a little, and there she was. Dead."

His pen traced words on the notepad and finished with a pronounced jab that I figured emphasized the word "DEAD".

"Did you touch the body?" Nichols asked.

"My hand might have grazed it as I unrolled the rug. I'm not sure."

"Okay. We'll have to get your fingerprints, unless they're already on file?" O'Brien cocked an inquisitive dark eyebrow at me.

"No, officer."

He made a note. "No worries. We'll get them."

I flexed my fingers. I always hoped I could stay out of the fingerprint database during my lifetime. Chalk up two firsts for today, and it wasn't even nine o'clock yet.

"I know who it is."

That got their attention. "Who is it?"

"Her name is Paige Whitaker," I said. "She worked in the office of the OceanScapes resort two blocks down. Ran their human resources."

"How do you know her?"

"She comes in here every couple of weeks. She liked mysteries of all sorts. Patricia Cornwell, Agatha Christie, and the like. She was a big fan of Hope Clarke."

"Sure," he said, not caring about the victim's reading preferences. "Know who might have done this?"

"No clue. I knew her but didn't know her well enough to have an idea of who would do such a thing. It's terrible. She came in here with her friends from work most of the time. She was a fun person to speak with."

O'Brien stared at me, chewed on his bottom lip, and closed his notepad. "Okay, I think I've got all from you I need for now. I'm sure the detectives will have you repeat what you told me to them when they get here and dive deeper. Try to remember anything out of the ordinary you may have seen on your way here. Even the tiniest detail might be important."

"I will."

"What time does your store open?"

"Ten. One of my employees, Karen, should be here any minute. What do you want me to do?"

He stepped around the corner and stared down the length

of the building, leaning to the side. "It's a fairly good distance from here to the front. We should be out of the way back here. It's up to you if you still want her to open at your regular time. We'll need you to be available later for further questioning."

"I'll do that."

"Hang around inside for now. Try to go about your business as usual. The detectives and medical examiners should be here soon." He regarded the gathering crowd. "We need to lock this scene down as much as we can and don't need you calling all of your friends and relatives to tell them what you found."

"Absolutely. I'll go around to the front and let myself in, if that's okay by you?"

"Yeah, man. That's fine."

I turned to walk away, and my shoe scuffed up against the box of pastries.

"Don't forget those," O'Brien said, "or Murph here will inhale them."

"Hey," the hefty firefighter said defensively, looking up from the body.

As I knelt down to pick up the box, Murph said, "O'Brien, check this out."

"Excuse us, Mr. Thomas," Nichols said, "but we need for you to go inside while we investigate."

"Yes, officer," I replied and walked away, but not before I saw what had interested them about Paige.

CHAPTER
TWO

The day had started as a normal Tuesday. I had grabbed an assortment of bagels and pastries from Benjamin's Bakery in Surfside. Rolled up Kings Highway with the window rolled down in my Jeep, enjoying the salty morning air, to my bookstore across from the southern tip of the Boardwalk.

Then everything went sideways.

I checked my phone as I walked around the side of the building and saw that I had one missed call from Karen before punching redial. I kept my waiting for my wife to call. I should stop expecting it after not getting one from her in two years.

Karen picked up after one ring.

"Hey," she said with a distinct Southern drawl. "What's going on here? Is everything all right?"

"You're here already?"

"Yeah," she said, her voice a pitch higher. "You know I live nearby. I was up and stirring when you called."

"Where are you right now?"

"I walked across the street on Ocean Boulevard. I'm standing here on the sidewalk."

The ocean came into view beyond the Boardwalk as I rounded the corner. Seagulls squawked. Karen stood on the other side of the street with one knee bent with a phone pressed against her ear. She waved. I motioned her to come across. After looking both ways, she waited as a black car inched past, the driver rubbernecking to see what was going on behind Myrtle Beach Reads.

She hurried across after the car passed and stepped up on the sidewalk next to me. Her mouth hung open. "What in the world, Clark?"

I hooked my thumb over my shoulder. "There's a dead person back there."

Both hands covered her mouth as she gasped. "You're kidding!"

"I wish I was."

"Who is it?" Her eyes kept flicking from me to the scene at the rear of the building and back to me.

"Paige from OceanScapes."

"No way. She was in here yesterday."

"She was?"

"Yeah. Said she was going on vacation, I guess, starting today," Karen said between quick breaths. She was on the verge of hyperventilating. "Wanted to pick up a few books."

Interesting. I gave her a quick, consoling hug while balancing the pastries in one hand. Her head barely reached my armpit. She shivered.

"Look," I said. "Let's get the coffee going. I've already spoken to the police. They told me to hang tight while they investigate."

Karen was in her late forties and had short blond hair tied back into a ponytail. She had designer pink-rimmed glasses. She lived her life in a perpetual chipper mood.

"What about the store?"

"They said we can open like normal. Can't go out the back door. I will need to speak to their homicide detectives at some point, though. So, I'll need you to hold down the fort when that happens. Have to cancel the Veteran's Coffee Hour."

"Bummer." She stared at the back corner of the store where people were gathering to watch. "Oh no, Clark. I can't believe this is happening. Were you the one who found her?"

"I was."

"That's terrible. For you and her. Especially her. What happened?"

I glanced over her shoulder at the increasing traffic on Ocean Boulevard. Most cars slowed when they reached us and saw the flashing red and blue lights at the rear of the store.

"Let's get inside, and then I'll tell you about it."

* * *

Our strip, formally called "The Shops on the Boardwalk", holds four businesses. It sat on the opposite side of the street from the Boardwalk. The location — as is imperative to the survival of any used bookstore — offered a sizeable amount of foot traffic.

The rent wasn't nearly as high as I figured when I queried the building owner years ago. She kept the rent increases reasonable as the years went by. We never had to scrimp to survive.

The building is a bright lime green to make it stand out to passersby. A covered walkway at the front allowed us to set out a few tables for patrons to sit and enjoy their coffee and books.

Besides our business, the building housed the Boardwalk

Creamery, I Heart MB Tees, and Coastal Décor. Patrons of the ice cream parlor on the far end of the building used our chairs, but I never shooed anyone away. It was more important to accommodate than be prickly. I didn't want to alienate potential customers as I kept a bargain rack outside the door under the overhang. We've had countless customers drop a few dog-eared paperbacks and hardcovers with red stickers on our counter from that rack while trying to keep melting ice cream from running down their cones.

I unlocked the door and allowed Karen to enter first. I went in after her, disabled the alarm, and glanced out to see a news truck lumbering up the street towards us. Yippee. Why did I feel that I'd get a camera shoved in my face? I lowered the blind.

I turned to my store. Four shelves of new releases faced customers as they entered. Our strategy in laying out the place was to have certain books up front to draw in customers but put the most wanted genres at the rear of the store. That way, they'd have to go through the entire store to get to what they wanted.

Hopefully, they would pick up a few books they didn't know they wanted along the way. Mysteries, Thrillers, Crime and Romance lined shelves at the rear of the store. The Young Adult section came before it. We had a big Thomas the Train wooden play table in the large Children's section.

Two counters sat on opposite sides of the store. One was for the cash register and computer that kept up with inventory. A shelf with requested items held for customers was behind that. The other counter was used to serve coffee. Six small white tables with two chairs apiece lay in between the counters.

Biography and Nonfiction sections flanked both sides of the New Release case. We scattered comfy seating throughout the store for people to browse, leaf through books, work on their laptops, or sip coffee.

It wasn't supposed to be this easy. Everyone cautioned my wife and I that owning our own business was hard work. We had stashed money away and had always dreamed of owning our own used bookstore. The plan was for Autumn to continue working her job at City Municipal Court until the business was profitable enough for her to quit.

Sure, from the day we conceived the idea, to the quiet opening of the bookstore were six of the most worrisome, sleepless, backbreaking, and challenging months of our lives. First, we had to find a perfect location. Then, after locating and securing that part, we had to find enough quality books to fill the shelves. That meant renting out a small storage unit at a local U-Store facility until we built the shelving and traveling over three states to find the right books.

While we did that, we envisioned the layout. The arrangement of the bookshelves and sitting areas. Did we want a coffee bar or treats for customers to enjoy while they sat and read? There was a myriad of factors to weigh before opening ten years ago.

As Karen went through the pre-opening checklist, I stepped behind the counter to the right of the door and pulled a sheet of blank paper from the copier. I reached in the drawer underneath the cash register and plucked out a blue magic marker and scrawled a note as well as I could on the paper.

Our Apologies, Veteran's Coffee
Canceled for this Week.

I examined it. Didn't like it and crumpled it into a ball.

"Hey Karen?" I called.

She poked her head out of the back office where she was getting the money ready for the cash drawer. "Yeah, Clark?"

"I need you to write a sign to hang on the door when you get a chance."

"Couldn't read your own, huh?"

She knew my penmanship, or lack thereof. She understood me. "You know it. When you get a chance."

We chose Tuesdays for the Vet's Coffee Hour because this day was the slowest of the week. The store opened at 10:00 every morning, except on Sundays when we unlocked the doors at noon.

I crossed to the other side and set the pastries on the coffee counter. Turning on the faucet with a squeak, I measured out twenty-four ounces of water into a pot and set it on the hot plate. As that came to a boil, I ground out forty-eight grams of coffee beans in a burr grinder on the coarse setting and shook it into the bottom of a French press.

Steam rose from the pot before coming to a rolling boil. I cut the heat and let the water come to a rest for thirty seconds. I mentally counted the time. At the end, I poured the water into the press. I counted another thirty to allow the grinds to bloom before giving it a stir. After placing the plunger in the press, I set a timer for four minutes.

I blew out a breath. Karen was still in the back where the clinking sounds of coins dropping into a register till emanated. She liked to have one cup of coffee in the morning. I arranged for my customary two.

I rarely started the mornings with a French press. On a normal day, I brewed an urn of coffee in the Bunn drip-maker. I changed it up today because a) I didn't know for sure when the store would open, and b) the process with the French press was cathartic, allowing me to calm my mind and place the events of the morning in perspective.

Before I had time to process things, someone tapped on the glass of the front entrance. Because I drew the shade, I couldn't see who it was. I walked up there a drew the blind aside to reveal a tall, caramel-skinned woman wearing a dark blue pantsuit with cerulean pinstripes. Her dark hair was pulled back in a tight bun. She looked official.

Her partner, not so much. He was short and stocky, with a flat nose and unkempt hair that hung down below his ears under a dilapidated tan trilby hat. His attire was like that of his partner's, just cheaper and ratty. He reminded me of a scruffy poodle.

She faced me and smiled, holding up a badge in her right hand. "Mr. Thomas?" she said, her voice muffled through the glass.

"Yes," I returned, flipping the deadbolt and opening the door. "Come on in."

I waved them through, and she shook my hand as she entered. Her grip was stronger than I expected. He had the grip of a dead fish. The fragrance of some unknown expensive perfume followed her inside. A stale cigarette odor followed him.

Her dark brown eyes regarded me for a moment. "Good morning, Mr. Thomas. I'm Detective Gina Gomez. This is my partner, Detective Phil Moody. Do you have few minutes to talk?"

I gestured at the dark, empty store. "I do."

"Good," she said with a tight smile.

The timer beeped behind the counter.

"Excuse me," I said.

I returned to the French press and plunged the coffee. They followed me and stopped on the other side of the counter. The lids of her eyes were heavy and the undersides puffy, like she was still shaking off the cobwebs of sleep. Moody looked like he was still asleep.

"Coffee?" I offered.

Gomez's ears lowered as she smiled. "Yes, I would like that," she said, peering over the hardwood counter. "Didn't have time to get any before I hopped in the car."

Moody grunted. "Same."

I grabbed four mugs from underneath the bar and filled them all with equal amounts. I handed her a steaming mug and pointed to my right, "There's sugar over there. Need cream?"

"No, black for me," she said and took a tentative sip. Her eyes closed as she savored the smoky brew from Central America.

Moody snorted. "Same."

I wanted to ask him if he was a Neanderthal but thought better of it.

I reached into the mini-fridge and took out a carton of half and half. Pouring a dollop into my mug, I called to Karen informing her the coffee was ready. I took a plastic spoon and stirred. The cream swirled and infused with the coffee, lightening it a shade. Just how I liked it. No sugar for me. Gave that up years ago.

As I came around the counter, I gestured the detectives to a table. Gomez drew a chair and sat. Moody turned another around backwards and straddled it like it was a motorcycle. I took a position across from Gomez, mug in hand.

She took a small recording device from her pocket and set it in the middle of the table. Moody sipped on his coffee. Then, she plucked a small notebook from her back pocket, similar to the one Officer O'Brien used. "Mind if I record this?"

"No, not at all," I said. I mean, what choice did I have in the matter?

Karen came out from the office and introduced herself to Gomez before preparing her coffee and disappearing again.

"I'll need to talk to her," Gomez said to me as Karen scurried away.

"No problem. Don't know what she can tell you, though. She only got here a couple minutes ago."

"If it's all the same, I'll decide what and how much she can tell me."

I sat up straight in my chair. Gomez didn't like people telling her how to do her job. Noted.

After registering our names, time, date, and location, she asked me to describe what I saw and how I discovered the body. "Leave out no details. I need to know who or what you saw coming and going. It's possible you saw the murderer leaving the scene but don't know it. Yet."

I closed my eyes for a moment, trying to gather the details.

"Let's see," I said, "I parked my Jeep on a lot back between Chester Street and 5th Avenue North. I grabbed a box of pastries and hopped out of the Jeep. A couple of the Myrtle Beach city trucks passed by on Ocean Boulevard. A beer truck rolled past me and turned right onto Flagg before lumbering down to one of the restaurants."

"Do you know which one?"

"I don't. It was too far away."

"Okay. Continue."

"Two golf carts from different motels crisscrossed in front of me."

"Do you recall which motels they were from?"

"I don't. They weren't those rental carts you see all the time during the summer."

Her mouth twitched and forehead puckered. "Okay. What else did you see?"

She didn't like my last response. I wasn't here to make her happy, I was just telling her what I knew. I told her about my interaction with Theresa of I Heart MB Tees. She scribbled something

I kept going. "It didn't look as though Sherry was in at Coastal Décor yet as I passed. Her business doesn't open until eleven." Gomez scrawled another note. "When I got to my alcove, I saw something laying there. It looked like a rolled-up carpet. But uneven."

"Then what did you do?"

"I reached down and unrolled it a bit and saw that it was a body."

She wrote a few notes, then said, "So the woman, Paige?"

"Yeah, Paige."

"The Paige from OceanScapes?"

"Yup."

Her lips tightened. "That's horrible. I knew of her. She did so much in the community."

"She's the one who organized a lot of the rallies about protecting the beaches and oceans, right?" Moody said.

"She is. Was," I said. "Had a big role in stamping out the

people who wanted to drill for oil offshore a couple years ago."

"I remember that now," Moody said.

"She led a couple rallies," I said. "Gave a speech at a county meeting. Even went to the capital building in Columbia to speak against it."

"That's right," Moody said. "Isn't she also the one behind trying to get a ban on plastic bags here like they did in North Myrtle Beach?"

"Yup." Gomez took a gulp of coffee. "I was at a cause she put together with first responders to raise awareness about that a couple months ago. I think it will get passed by the city council sooner rather than later."

"That's good," I said. "I switched to paper bags in my store when North Myrtle put their ban on plastic bags into effect."

Her lips tightened, probably thinking the same thing I was. Myrtle Beach lost an influential person.

"So, you say Paige was getting ready to leave for vacation?"

"That's what Karen told me," I said.

She pointed a finger at me. "Karen might not tell me much or anything about the body, but she can help give context. There's more to solving a murder than forensics. Many times, it's the smallest details that come together that provide us with a clear picture of what happened."

I'd read enough murder mysteries to realize that was true. To me, the best whodunits were the ones solved through old-fashioned detective skills. Finding leads, chasing leads, putting pieces of the puzzle together.

"I was wrong. I apologize."

The corners of her eyes crinkled. "No worries." She studied her notes.

Moody jumped in and pointed a finger at my chest. "Mr. Thomas, can you prove to us where you were before finding the body?"

CHAPTER
THREE

The question caught me off guard. Until this point, we'd had an amiable conversation. Almost friendly as Gomez guided me through the events with an almost sympathetic manner. Then Moody lives up to his name and changed the tone. I gulped as I considered how to answer.

What was their point of view? They came in cold, with little information to go on. They learned the name of the victim from me. Why wouldn't they suspect me as the murderer? I could have killed Paige, rolled her up in that rug, placed her at the back landing, and called it in like someone else did the deed.

I realized that I might have taken too long to respond.

Moody scowled.

"Look, I have a receipt with a time stamp." I pulled the thin paper out of my left pocket and handed it to him. Gomez leaned over to study the receipt.

"The time stamp clears him, Detective," Gomez said.

Moody snorted and stuffed the paper into a jacket pocket. "We'll see. I'll head down there later and verify this."

Gomez cleared her throat. "Moving on. Do you have any enemies, business rivals?"

I stuck out my lower lip. "Not that I know of."

She uncrossed her arms. "I'm aware of your reputation, Mr. Thomas. You're a respectable member of the business community. Seems like I always see your business's name attached to various charitable causes."

My cheeks flushed. "Thanks. We try. I think I have a good relationship with most locals. I try to treat everyone well."

"Any spats or confrontations with anyone recently?"

"Nope."

Someone tapped on the glass door. She clicked off the tape recorder and closed her notebook. We stood. She drained the last dregs of her coffee and said, "I think that's all I need for now, Mr. Thomas."

I held up a hand. "No, please, call me Clark. My dad is Mr. Thomas."

She smiled. "Sure thing, Clark."

She handed me her empty mug, and I reached over and set it on the other side of the counter. Moody left his mug on the table. Brown splatters surrounded it. Still cradling my coffee, we walked to the front door where I pushed the blind aside to find O'Brien standing outside.

"Hey Gomez," he said, his voice slightly muffled through the glass. "Need you back here."

"We're coming." She turned to me. "Tell Ms. Cline that we will be back to question her." She reached into a pocket and handed me a card. "My info is on there. Call me if you think of anything."

I took the card. "Thanks. I will."

I unlocked the door and held it open so she could exit. She brushed past me in a hurry and joined O'Brien as they rushed around the side of the building. The smell of her perfume lingered. Moody tagged along behind her. He grunted as he passed.

The sun had completed its ascent in the sky out over the ocean across the street. Palm trees swayed in a gentle onshore breeze carrying the salty smell in with it. It was shaping up to be a pleasant Chamber of Commerce type day here on the Boardwalk. Except for the murder, that is.

I sensed a motion to my right on the walkway. I turned and saw a man named Kyle ambling this way. I'm not sure what his last name was. He's one of the vets who comes every week for Coffee Hour.

"Morning, Mr. Thomas," he said with a raspy voice.

"Morning, Kyle. Sorry man, no coffee hour this morning. Have to cancel this week."

He regarded me with a blank look. He gave a half-smile, revealing two rows of crooked teeth. "That's okay. I've got plenty to do on my plate today."

I knew it would disappoint him. "Hold up here for a sec." I held up a finger. I rushed back in and came out a moment later with the pastry box from Benjamin's.

"Here, these were for you guys. Take them."

"Thank you." He opened the lid and licked his lips. "Hey, what happened back there? What's all the commotion about?"

I hooked a thumb at the rear of the building. "Found someone dead this morning."

"Oh man. That sucks. Who was it?"

"Paige from down at OceanScapes."

He furrowed a brow. "Don't think I know her. Feel bad for her family and her. And you for finding it, matter of fact. Seeing a dead body is never a pleasant thing. I remember the first one I saw in 'Nam. He was my best friend. Childhood buddies. We enlisted together and somehow ended up at the same base at Camp Evans."

My heart fell. "I feel your pain."

He seemed to fumble for the words. "I remember, Mr. Thomas."

We faced each other in an awkward silence. A lone pelican flew past the shops, angling for the ocean.

"Listen," I said. "Gotta run."

"I understand, Mr. Thomas."

Why did people insist on calling me that? Kyle was old enough to be my father. "You know you can call me Clark, don't you?"

"I do, but you're someone I respect. Therefore, you're Mr. Thomas to me."

I could see that I would not change his mind. I waved. "Have a great day, Kyle. See you next week?"

He started shuffling backwards. "God willing." He turned and started walking to points unknown.

I stared after his receding back. I couldn't put myself in his shoes, nor in anyone else's. I've learned that death is not evil. It is the only law free of discrimination. Everyone dies. Most don't get to choose when.

Kyle's friend probably didn't wake up that morning knowing he wouldn't see the end of it. Paige certainly didn't choose her fate. What caused someone to knock her on the head? How did she end up here? Why did she end up here? Was someone trying to frame me?

"Hey Clark, can you step back here for a moment?" Gomez motioned me back to the alcove.

I rounded the corner and took my time getting there. I didn't particularly want to see Paige's body again and didn't know if they had time to move it yet. Yellow police tape was strung from the corner of the building to the light pole on the corner and connected back to the building on the other side of Coastal Décor. A van from the coroner's office had wedged itself between the police and fire vehicles with direct access to the body.

That was such an odd and macabre way to think about someone I knew. "The body." I shivered despite the pleasant temperature.

Two other officers had arrived to keep the onlookers at bay. There were a dozen or so people milling about, trying to glimpse what was going on. The word was out now, especially as news crews from two separate television stations were preparing to shoot.

One officer greeted me with a nod and raised the tape. I ducked and stepped around the corner. I breathed a sigh of relief when I saw that the body and rug were gone. Crime scene investigators were busy snapping photos and taking measurements. One of them had drawn a boxy chalk outline on the gray cement on the right side of the stoop, depicting where I found Paige. Moody stood in a corner of the alcove, writing something on a notepad. I imagined him drawing pictures of kitty cats.

"One question," Gomez said to me and pointed to the rear corner of the bay above the metal door. "Do you have access to the feed on that camera?"

I had forgotten about the surveillance camera. I installed it several years ago. It was supposed to deter would-be thieves when delivery people left boxes back here.

"I do, but there's one problem."

"What's that?"

"That camera has a narrow field of vision. It only shows half of this recess. I doubt you'll even be able to see the body."

She rolled her eyes.

"Listen," I defended myself, "money was tight when we opened and had a few cases of books stolen early on. I bought one of those self-install cameras as a solution. It wasn't the best one. It basically shows the door and a few feet beyond it."

"Show me how far it goes."

I backed up about to about three feet from the door. I pointed at the ground in an arc in front of me. Two feet short of where the body once lay. "It goes out to about here."

Gomez, O'Brien, and Nichols all had the same expression and probably uttered the same curses under their breaths. Moody grunted. After expelling a long breath, Gomez said, "Okay. I still want to see that video."

"We can do that anytime. Let me know when you're ready."

She eyeballed me with a hint of suspicion. Here was a key moment. If she truly thought I might be a suspect, she would ask to see the video right now so I wouldn't have time to delete or edit it.

"We'll do that shortly," she said and studied the small, black camera. The index finger of her right hand curled over her lips. Then something changed her train of thought. "Look, Clark, I meant to tell you earlier not to speak to the media—and they will come with questions—until we make an official statement. And maybe not even then. I'll let you know."

I wasn't comfortable in front of a camera. I've been on

television before and interviewed by the local press. The newspaper interviews weren't so bad. Having a microphone and camera with a bright light stuck in your face and having you describe one of the worst events of your life is downright uncomfortable. It's not like you can practice something like that unless you work in the profession.

"Don't have to worry about that."

She placed a hand on my shoulder. "Look, Mr. Thomas."

"It's Clark."

She smiled. "Yes, I'm sorry. Clark, look, you went through something no one ever should in finding Paige like that. My advice to you is, go home, call some friends, get together, have a few beers, and try to forget about all this."

I looked down and brushed a few pebbles aside with my foot. A small cloud of dust and sand swirled. There's a large, grassy lot behind the Shops on the Boardwalk structure. It occurred to me that I've never seen anyone mow it. How did the owner keep the grass so short?

I would have rather let my mind wander than reply to her. Just stared off into space until Gomez got tired of waiting for a response and went about her business.

I whistled a short, vacant tune before responding. "Nah. That's okay. I don't really have any friends to call. All I do is work. This store is my life. Working takes my mind off everything."

If someone said those words to me, I would have the same sad look Gomez gave me now.

She clicked her tongue. "Alright."

"Was there anything else you needed me for?"

"That was it," Gomez said. "Just wanted to know about the

camera."

I pointed at the steel door in the alcove. "Knock on that door. Karen or I will come get you."

"Will do." She tapped a finger against her chin.

Gomez turned and spoke with Moody. I assumed that was a dismissal. I ducked under the yellow tape again and walked back to front of the store.

My brain flitted between a dozen different things as I walked. I jumped when someone said, "Excuse me?"

A tall woman with long brown hair was hurrying to catch up to me from the throng of onlookers. A guy with a scraggly gray beard trailed behind her with a large video camera perched on his shoulder.

"Excuse me?" she repeated.

I glanced back at the officers controlling the crowd, hoping one of them or Gomez would come rescue me. I didn't want to be on camera again. "Yes, can I help you?"

A toothy smile ran across her face. "Hi, I'm Erica Sullivan from WMHF News Channel 2, Myrtle Beach. Can I ask you a few questions?"

She wore a pair of faded blue jeans under a blue light jacket with the WMHF station logo and a big number two embroidered upon it. We shook hands. Her palm was sweaty. Don't know if it was because of the jacket or nervousness.

"Sure, but I don't know what I can tell you."

"Um, well, we got a tip that police were inspecting a possible crime scene here. That someone may have gotten shot. Can you tell me what happened here?"

I hesitated. "I can't really comment on it until they tell me I can."

She took a step back. A foot rapidly tapped on the sidewalk as she contemplated her next question. The cameraman gazed at the ocean across the street like he'd much rather be there instead of here. Couldn't blame him. He was probably tired of having to coddle young reporters fresh out of journalism school.

"What's your name?" she asked.

"Clark Thomas," I said.

"Cool." Her head bobbed as she made a note in her phone. Eyes of coal studied me. I was ready to escape back inside. "Did someone die here?"

I opened my mouth to answer, thought about it, and said, "No, no one died here."

It was the truth. Paige didn't die here. I thought it was a smart response. A little cagey, but smart. The murderer killed her somewhere else and dropped her here.

"Did you find a body?"

I had to give this young woman credit. She was sharp. I don't like to lie. The story would come out eventually. "Yes, I did."

She and her cameraman shared a look. He brought his camera up and pointed it at my face. She stood straighter and held the microphone to her chin. She broke the ice, but I would not let her carve any deeper. Not without permission from Gomez.

I held up my hand. "That's all I can say. I'm not going on camera."

Her shoulders sagged. The cameraman lowered the camera and returned his gaze to the ocean. He didn't care. He's probably seen it all.

Nonplussed, she said, "When do you think you can talk?"

"I don't know that I will, to be honest. I'd rather not appear on camera."

"I could ask you some questions off-camera. I wouldn't reveal your name."

I stared into her eyes to glean her truthfulness. She didn't blink or look away. "Tell you what, the police said not to talk to anyone until they release a statement. After they do, come back. We'll talk. Off camera."

"Deal."

We parted. My mind whirled as I headed back inside. Would the video feed show anything? Why didn't I go through the rear door and save myself this encounter? Sheesh, it's going to be a long day.

CHAPTER
FOUR

Karen loaded the register with money while I got the Bunn coffeemaker percolating.

During the busy summer season, we brewed four different types of coffee. A light roast, medium roast, dark roast, and a flavored coffee. Enough foot traffic came in that we rarely had to discard stale coffee. When the tourist season slowed, we only kept a medium roast to suit most coffee drinkers. It was that Goldilocks philosophy: not to light, not too dark, but just right.

Today's coffee came from Grand Strand Roasters out of Pawley's Island.

A few customers milled outside the front entrance as I flipped the sign to OPEN, unlocked the door and let them in. I didn't recognize any of them. Must be tourists.

They seemed unaware of the crime scene around back and entered like anyone else. Instrumental jazz played through hidden speakers in the ceiling.

I didn't feel like sitting in the office and allowing the morning's events to take over my mind. I would rather distract myself with work. You can find some interesting conversations with out-of-towners. That was one aspect I loved about owning this business.

Over the next little bit, I checked out a customer, served coffee, and had a pleasant conversation with two retirees from Maryland. This was their first visit to Myrtle Beach. A time share company gifted them a free weekend in exchange for sitting through a sales pitch.

They arrived the previous evening and were scheduled to tour the time share later this afternoon. I cautioned them not to allow the salesperson to fleece them with strong-arm tactics. I've heard many horror stories about what these companies do to lure in new victims, er, customers.

I was ringing up a dog-eared copy of an old Nora Roberts mystery to a woman from Ohio when I saw two familiar faces walk through the door. They worked at OceanScapes. One of them might be the perfect person to speak to. I wasn't sure about the other.

I stuffed a Myrtle Beach Reads bookmark in the bag with the woman's receipt and wished her a great day. The women from OceanScapes were perusing the latest issues at the magazine rack. I wanted to go over there, but a guy wearing a heavy sweater and Bermuda shorts called me over to the Sci-Fi section to ask me about Arthur C. Clarke books.

I placed a copy of Beyond the Fall of Night—one of my favorites from my teenage years—in the customer's hand, and hustled over to the coffee bar and prepared two café Americanos for a couple.

Before too long, the OceanScapes employees stood across the counter. They were a contrasting pair. The short one, Gloria, had dark skin and spiky hair and talked a mile a minute. The other, Natasha, was tall, blonde and had a pale complexion. She didn't talk much but spoke with a Russian accent when she did.

They always came into the store together.

"Ha ha, hey," Gloria said. She almost always greeted me with a laugh. That's the way she was. She placed a copy of the most recent Oprah magazine on the counter. "Thanks for helping me set up my new phone the other day."

"Oh, no problem."

Natasha stood quietly with a hand over a wrist.

Gloria had bought a new Android phone off eBay but didn't have a clue how to get a SIM card in it or how to use it.

She said, "I hate dealing with the salespeople in the stores. They always seem so condescending to me, and I appreciate you taking the time to help me out. And I don't have anyone else to help with my husband overseas and kids out on the West Coast. How's it going?"

An odd question, considering the circumstances. "Oh, busy as usual. I'm sorry about Paige."

"What about Paige?" Gloria asked.

"About her death," I whispered.

Their jaws dropped. Gloria placed a hand on the counter. "What are you talking about? Paige? She's not dead. I saw her yesterday."

"Uh, do you not know?"

"Know what?"

"I figured you would. I discovered Paige dead by my backdoor."

Gloria recoiled and put a hand over her mouth to stifle a shout. Natasha put a steadying arm around Gloria.

I came around the counter and led both women over to one table. Karen was straightening books on a shelf in the romance section and saw who I was speaking with. We shared a look and she took over behind the counter.

"Oh, no," Natasha said after we were seated.

"I'm sorry," I said. "It wasn't my place to tell you about it."

"Someone would have told us," Natasha said.

I got up and reached behind the coffee counter for a box of tissues and set them down before Gloria. Where she took the news hard, Natasha's face was expressionless, but her complexion had paled. She rubbed a hand on Gloria's upper back. After a minute, Gloria straightened and pulled herself together.

"That must be why they called us here this morning." Natasha sniffled. "To tell us about this. We were all standing around. After a while, they said we could leave, but not to go too far. So, we came here."

We sat in silence while they processed the news. Natasha still held her gaze on me. Her big, brown eyes made me squirm.

"She was such a sweet person," Gloria said. "I think she's worked there since OceanScapes opened."

"How long ago was that?"

"About twenty years," Gloria responded. "I've worked there for over a decade. She's the person who hired me."

"How many people work there?"

Gloria was doing all the talking. "There's thirty or so, I think."

HR was a bear of a task with my three employees. I couldn't imagine the time it took Paige to do that for an entire resort staff.

"Did she keep regular hours?"

"No. She was there at all times of the day, but popped in and out. Her office was in the management section upstairs, so we never saw when she came or left."

"So, no one could be sure when she'd be there?"

"No, not really."

"She was in here yesterday and told one of my employees she had a vacation that was supposed to start today. I wonder why she was at OceanScapes?"

"Maybe she was going to meet the murderer there. It got heated, and he ended up killing her," Gloria suggested.

"That's possible," I said, not knowing if it was or not. "Maybe they were up to something illegal, and the killer needed to cover his tracks."

Gloria pointed a finger. "Assuming that it was a he."

"True," I conceded. "Let's presume she was there for work-related reasons."

"It's a pay week," Natasha said. "Perhaps she was working on that."

"Like payroll and stuff?" I said.

"Yeah. We have computers and tablets everywhere," Gloria said. "But they still have the old paper timecards and time clocks to punch in and out on. I have no idea why they never upgraded to a computer or tablet to clock in." Her phone rang. She pulled it from her back pocket and looked at the screen. "It's work." She answered, said a few words, and ended the call. "We've been summoned."

I guided them to the front of the store. Gloria exited first while Natasha lagged behind. The door closed and Gloria was already bounding down the two steps to the sidewalk when Natasha turned to me.

She touched me on the wrist. A shiver ran up my arm. "I need to speak with you."

"Sure. What about?"

"It's Paige. I may know something. You keep your finger on the pulse of the Boardwalk, and I think you can help me."

She had me there. I liked knowing what was going on around my business, even if it meant poking into crevices I should probably keep my nose out of. "Oh, what do you know?"

"Can't talk now. Have to go, but I will return soon."

Why she would want to talk to me of all people? That's what the police were for. I reached in my back pocket and handed her a business card. "Here, take this. Call me if you need to."

She glanced at the card and back to me. "Thank you. I will do so."

Gloria called for Natasha from halfway down the block.

She left without another word, leaving me to wonder what she knew and why she needed to speak to me about it.

CHAPTER
FIVE

I told Karen I would be back in a few minutes and exited through the front door. Several cars were parked in the paid parking lot across the street. An older couple cruised by on rented bikes, their gray hair billowing out from under white ball caps. Waves crashed in the distance.

The front door to I Heart MB Tees was propped open, inviting customers inside. A wave of cool air greeted me as I stepped through the entrance and saw Theresa, the owner, alone in the store, flipping through a book on her counter. Racks of multi-colored shirts filled the bulk of the floor space in the store. Kitschy trinkets adorned the walls. I could say one thing about Theresa, she didn't waste any space. She filled almost every square inch of the business with something she could make money from.

Her ashy blonde hair was pulled back in a ponytail so tight that it was as if she had a built-in facelift. The amount of red makeup on her cheeks approached clownish levels. She perpetually smelled like a mixture of cheap perfume and an ash tray. She wore a white "I Heart Myrtle Beach" t-shirt above skin-tight cheetah print pants. She was a hardcore hippie during the 60's and never quite left it all behind. She was not a person I wanted to see this morning. Or any morning.

She has the hots for me.

"Heeeeyy, Clark," she drawled, looking up from the catalogue on her counter. Her voice sounded like the machine they use to scrape asphalt off the road. Probably from the years of smoking twelve packs a day. That's an estimate based on the fact that the only time I didn't see her with a lit cigarette hanging out of one corner of her mouth was when she was inside her store where it was illegal to smoke. I wouldn't put it past her, though, to sneak one from time to time.

"Good morning, Ms. Trask. How are you today?" Not that I cared, but I had an agenda here and needed to be sociable.

"I'm doing good, baby. Are you going to that meeting tonight?"

The city manager called for a meeting to discuss the future of downtown Myrtle Beach. A plan was set in motion several years ago, but with the local population growing at such a rapid pace and a change in the city to county distribution of the hospitality tax, city leaders felt that it was time to reevaluate the plan.

"Maybe. I want to see what they say, but I might be busy."

She looked me up and down in a manner that made me feel uncomfortable. I didn't want to think about what rabbit hole her mind went down when I said I would be busy.

"I'm sure you have some good ideas on how to use this extra tax money."

"Perhaps. I want to see what others have to say first." I walked back to her counter, bumping into a few racks of tightly packed kitschy t-shirts along the way.

"They're raising the prices on these Savvy Colors shirts,"

she said while chomping on a wad of gum. "They used to be cheaper than the bigger manufacturers. Now they're almost as expensive."

Theresa had most of her shirts custom made. She came up with the slogans and designs and sent them off to a printer in Concord, North Carolina to produce them. Some of her shirts were tacky, but others were nice, and if I didn't already live here, I'd buy them myself.

"That's capitalism for you," I said. "Make a good product and adjust your pricing as you realize where you fit in the market."

She blew a bubble until it popped. "Yeah, doesn't help small business owners like me, though."

"Do you sell more of that brand of shirt than others?"

She looked at the ceiling and cocked her head to one side. "I do. The difference in quality is noticeable when you're picking through the racks. People buy those over others."

"Well, there you go. If you had a store full of sub-quality clothing, your sales might not be as good."

"True," she conceded. "But you know these tourists will buy about anything with the words 'Myrtle Beach' on them."

"That's true too."

She regarded me with a wary eye. "You rarely come over here for small talk, sweet cheeks. What's up?"

"When you were working out back earlier, throwing away boxes, did you see anything suspicious?"

Her eyebrows knitted together, and the corners of her mouth lowered. She blew a bubble and popped it. "Suspicious? What do you mean?"

"Right before I came by this morning. Did you see anything

down on my end?"

"No. Why?"

I expelled a breath. "I found a body by my door."

A hand shot up to her mouth. "You're joking, right?"

"Apparently the killer dropped it off a few minutes before I got here."

The skinny hand lowered to a spot below her neck. "Oh no. No, I don't remember seeing anything. I was breaking down boxes and stacking them up."

"When did you get here?"

"I came in before seven and started working on my delivery from yesterday after that. You don't think I had anything to do with it, do you?"

Theresa was all skin and bones. She had asked me to come over several times to help her move boxes that were too heavy for her. She wasn't strong enough to carry around a body rolled up in a rug.

"No, of course not. Just curious about if you saw anything. Has anyone talked to you yet?"

"No."

"They probably will. I told them I saw you out back as I was coming in."

"Who is it? Was it?"

I jerked a thumb in the door's direction. It wasn't too important to keep quiet about it to Theresa. She'd find out soon enough. "It was that Paige lady who worked in the office down at OceanScapes."

"I'm not familiar with her."

The owner of OceanScapes, John Curtis, is a member of the Myrtle Beach Downtown Development Corporation, like

Teresa. We all attended the same monthly meetings to discuss how to make our area of Myrtle Beach grow and keep attracting tourists. I shot him a text earlier to pass along my condolences. I may have jumped the gun there.

"She was a nice woman. Do you remember seeing anything before I got here?"

"Why are you asking? Are you a cop now?"

I forced a laugh. "No, curious is all."

"Hmm. Just the usual traffic. A few cars. A few trucks. The odd golf cart or two."

"Anyone come by on foot?"

"Not that I recall. Are they still out there? The police?"

"They were the last time I checked."

She glanced at her rear door. "I'm going to go check it out." She left without another word, leaving me alone in an empty store.

I shrugged and exited the same way I entered.

CHAPTER
SIX

I returned to my office, shut the door, and leaned back against it. Karen could handle the store for a few minutes.

This was the first quiet moment I've had since waiting for the police after calling in the body. I lifted my glasses off the bridge of my nose and ran my hands over my face. Two days worth of stubble bristled against my palms. I didn't shave as often as I used to.

Light streamed in from a window set high on the wall against a cluttered bookshelf stocked with writing manuals, books on writing, and how-to's on book marketing. Some were helpful. Most were not, but I still held on to them in case they held some kernel of information that I might find useful someday.

There's an unfinished manuscript burning a hole in my hard drive that's due in two weeks. That is what I should have been doing instead of finding a dead body. The latest in an action-adventure series I ghostwrite. The author whose name graces the cover is getting up in years and he doesn't write many books anymore. He has several spinoff series under his brand. I write the first draft of a novel of one of those spinoffs after the story runners draft an outline. While I get no credit for the writing, I get some nice royalty checks and get to travel to faraway places while doing research. The pursuit of fame never intrigued me, but I don't mind the perks.

I was running ahead of schedule on it, so it shouldn't be too difficult to meet the deadline.

Before I assimilated the morning's events, a metallic tap emanated from the backdoor. It was Gomez and Moody. After showing them to the office, Gomez sat on the other side of the desk, one long leg folded over the other. She pressed a hand to her face and squeezed her eyes shut, exposing worry lines on her forehead. I couldn't imagine how stressful her job must be. Moody closed the office door behind him and stood against it.

They declined my offer for more coffee and preferred to get down to business. I fired up my computer and waited for the security software to load.

"Do you want to watch from over here?" I offered.

She pulled her chair around and sat close to me so we could share the screen. Moody stayed in place. He couldn't have much of a view from there, but whatever. The playback instructions were easy enough to explain. She could have asked to view it by herself but didn't.

"I'm sorry," I said. "It's an old computer and takes its sweet time to load."

She batted a hand. "Meh, you should see the relics we have at the station. Mine still has a floppy disk drive."

My eyebrows rose. "You're kidding?"

"Nope. It's like they'll spend most their budget on some things and skimp on others. Boys and their toys, you know? I guess as long as my computer will still boot up, they won't replace it."

"That's not optimal."

"Yeah, it is what it is. I don't use it much anyway. Just to write up reports."

"I see," I said as if I understood all the facets of her job. I placed my right hand on the mouse to move the cursor around the screen.

The fabric of her pantsuit rustled against the seat as she leaned forward, eyes intent on the screen. Her perfume smelled like a delicate unknown tropical flower. She crossed her right leg over her left knee. Her foot brushed against my knee. She jerked it back. "Sorry," she said.

"No worries," I said. "Close quarters." I clicked on the security program. "Here we go."

We watched as a box appeared on the monitor. I enlarged it to fit the screen. "It's basic," I said. "Everything gets saved to a hard drive I keep below the desk."

"What do you do when a drive gets filled?"

"They don't. Videos over twenty-eight days old automatically get deleted."

Her chin dipped. "Makes sense."

"Besides, it's not like there's much to see with the camera's limited field of vision."

Looking at the feed, she said, "True."

I brought up the video from this morning. "I called you all right after I discovered Paige, and the clock on the phone said it was a minute before eight. So, I'll go back before that."

"Her body was still warm when you found it," she said. "She couldn't have been there long. Go back to about five. Let's see if we pick up anything."

The camera showed a narrow view of the alcove from a

corner above the door through a fisheye lens. The image got distorted at the fringes of the video and enlarged in the center. When the scene first appeared, it showed crime scene investigators in real time, combing over the alcove. I slid the time dial back on the feed and the characters moved, in reverse motion. Gomez had me stop at a point before they took Paige's body away. As I suspected, only the front edge of the rug and Paige were visible. Gomez groaned knowing that this might be a futile task.

She had me resume rewinding. I first appeared around the 7:52 mark. My head and shoulders were visible on the screen. Everything below that wasn't. It was odd to watch myself talking on the phone to the 911 dispatcher. Still going backwards through time, we watched as I unrolled a corner of the rug to reveal Paige's face.

I kept the feed moving. Glow from a light above the door shined on the space. It was on a timer and shut off at six every morning. The sunlight coming in dimmed as the time kept receding, leaving the alcove porchlight as the only source of luminescence.

The rug containing Paige first appeared at 7:48. I imagined hearing the thump it made as it came to rest.

The body had been there less than five minutes before I appeared. Goosebumps raised on my arms.

"Ugh," Gomez sighed. "Nothing."

"Sorry," I apologized. It's not like I didn't warn her of the outcome. At least this seemed to prove that I wasn't the one who deposited her body here.

"It would have been nice to have whoever dumped the body walk up to the camera, smile and wave. Make my job much easier."

"Does that happen much? A crook does something stupid and gets themselves caught?"

She shifted. "You'd be surprised."

"Hmm. I guess that's why those Dumb Crook News websites exist."

"Yeah, it's scary how dumb some people are."

I pointed at the screen. "What about this person? The killer, not Paige."

Her brows drew together. "Not much to go on. I'm assuming the killer is male because of the strength needed to transport a body in a rug. The victim, in this case, didn't weigh much. It would still take a good amount of strength to do this."

"Could have been two women."

She leaned away from me and put a hand on her cheek. "That hadn't occurred to me."

"Yeah, what if a couple women had reason to kill Paige and did this together?"

"It's a possibility. I'll make a note of it. What was your impression of her?"

"She was pleasant. Always seemed to have a smile on her face."

"Is that all?"

"She was well put together. Seemed like she had her life in order."

"What makes you say that?"

"She always appeared well-dressed."

"She dressed well. What else?"

"She had an excellent memory. She could recall conversations we had about books long after they occurred.

Like, I would suggest something for her to read related to another book she'd have in her hands and she'd come back months later asking for it by name."

"Anything else?"

"She was a delightful conversationalist. Had a good vocabulary."

"Can you think of any reason why anyone would kill her?"

"Not really."

We sat in silence for a moment, both watching the monitor and the front edge of the rug sitting on the floor of the rear alcove. Moody came over and looked at the feed but said nothing.

"Actually," I said, "now that I think about it, there is a group out there that might have it out for her."

"Who is that?"

"Remember a couple years ago when those corporations tried to get offshore drilling passed here?"

"I do." The President loosened regulations on searching for oil along the coast and several companies won permission to conduct seismic testing off the coast of South Carolina. The environmental impact could wreak havoc on the beaches and marshlands in the state and have a tremendous impact on tourism. "It upset me when I heard about it. Wasn't Paige front-and-center of the pushback around here?"

I nodded. "She was. I was at a rally she organized against it."

"Me too."

"Then we might have seen each other there."

I recalled the events of that evening. A prominent U.S. Senator flew in and delivered an impassioned speech against drilling.

I asked, "Do you know if she received any death threats from that?"

"I'm not sure, but I wouldn't discount it. Sometimes those companies hire thugs to intimidate groups against them. I'll check into that."

"I wouldn't put it past them."

Gomez studied her notepad, tapping her pen against the side of the table. "Listen, I have all I need from you at present. If anything else comes up, I'll let you know. I know there's going to be media types wanting to speak with you."

"Already has."

"Figures. They're aggressive, I'll give them that. Anyway, don't talk to them until I give you word. I'll shoot you a text."

She looked at a silver watch on her wrist. "Give us another hour. Gotta dust for prints. Take pictures. That kind of thing. We'll have to get yours and your employees' prints so we can eliminate them from the scene."

"Thanks," I said, but didn't mean it.

Gomez couldn't think of anything else to ask and stood. Moody left with a grunt. I rose with her in the cramped quarters. We were a few inches apart. I was trapped against the wall and couldn't create more space. A sympathetic smile formed.

"I remember you now," she said. Her breath was warm as it blew against my face.

I grimaced. "Yeah. I had hoped no one would be able to place me, but I guess there was no getting out of it."

She reached up and put a hand on my shoulder. "I'm sorry about your wife's passing."

CHAPTER
SEVEN

My heart sunk and I stared at the space between our feet. She had nice shoes. Mine were scuffed and worn. Every day was tough. Especially considering the circumstances of my wife's death.

I looked away for a moment before meeting her eyes. "No, it's okay. It's been two years now. Can't say I'll ever be fine, but life goes on, you know?"

"Yeah, I do."

"I guess someone in your position would."

"Unfortunately." She removed her hand. She left me to myself and I reflected on poor Paige's fate and why Gomez had gotten so sympathetic there at the end.

* * *

By noon, most of the onlookers were gone, as was half of the police presence. Crime scene investigators remained to comb over the scene. I placed a handwritten sign out back for deliveries to be brought through the front door. If anyone could read it, that is. I wasn't expecting any today, but I'd already had one surprise delivery this morning.

I received a text from Gomez informing me they had put out a statement and to be prepared for the press. Great.

A minute later, I was back in my office. I pulled up the local news from a streaming service on my computer. I caught it as they were returning from a commercial break.

A "Breaking News" graphic in bold, red letters flashed across the screen. A middle-aged blonde anchor with shoulder-length hair sat behind a silver news desk reading from a teleprompter. The chyron at the bottom of the screen read, "DEATH ON THE BOARDWALK."

It wasn't quite on the Boardwalk. More like beside it.

"One local business owner," she reported, "found a surprise waiting by his backdoor as he arrived to work this morning. Clark Thomas, owner of Myrtle Beach Reads, discovered the body of Paige Whitaker rolled up in a rug on the landing behind the backdoor of his business shortly before eight."

I crossed my fingers, hoping that they wouldn't talk about the last time my name was mentioned in the news.

The screen cut to Detective Gomez standing in front of a throng of reporters outside of the police department. She stood erect with her chin held high. A touch of scarlet brought out her cheekbones, highlighted by dark red lipstick that she wasn't wearing this morning. Moody stood next to her. It was probably good that Gomez stood in front of the microphones instead of her partner. He'd probably grunt his way through the statement, caveman style.

"We are gathering evidence and speaking to potential witnesses," Gomez said. "We have a few early leads that we are exploring."

That caught my attention. What leads had they uncovered?

Did I point them in a direction, or did they find some evidence on the landing that told them something? Maybe they dug up something on one of those offshore drilling companies. Even more alarming: was I the lead?

The camera cut to footage of the outside of the bookstore where police were investigating earlier this morning.

"Whitaker was a long-time employee at the OceanScapes resort a few blocks south of where her body was found," the anchor said, her voice coming over images of the crime scene, the stately OceanScapes tower, and the Boardwalk as seen from the beach with the SkyWheel as the centerpiece. "The murder is only the second to occur within Myrtle Beach city limits this year. The other happened back in March when twenty dollars was stolen from the tip jar of a taco truck doing business outside of the convention center.

"Police tell us that Whitaker's death resulted from blunt force trauma to the head. No motive is known at this time. We will keep you updated on this story as we learn more."

I logged off the computer and laced my fingers behind my head, figuring that it was only a matter of time before that reporter from WMHF returned now that the police made their statement. I hoped she would forget about me, but I doubted that would be the case.

I didn't have to wait long for someone to get back to me, but it wasn't the reporter.

Karen stuck her head in my office with one hand on the doorframe. "Clark, you have a visitor."

"Thank you, Karen. Show them in."

She stepped aside to allow Natasha to enter. It wasn't every day that I had visitors in my office. Now she was the second. I squirmed in my chair and halfway stood to greet her.

"Hello again." I gestured at a chair on the other side of the desk. "Please, have a seat."

Her brown eyes traveled around the office before sitting. "Thank you for speaking to me."

"Of course," I said. "How can I help you?"

"I might know something about Paige."

I sat up straight in my chair. "Have you spoken to the police about it?"

She waved a hand. "No, no. I cannot speak to them about this."

I cocked my head. "Why not?"

"Because I am scared."

Now she had my attention. "Scared of what? Someone you work with?"

"Scared might be the incorrect word. Hmm. Distrustful is the word I'm looking for."

"Why don't you trust the police?"

"It goes back to where I come from."

"Where is that?"

"Moldova. The police there are corrupt, incompetent, and prone to mistreating suspects and prisoners."

"Are you a suspect?"

She bit her lip. "No, but someone might say something to suggest that."

"Why do you think that?"

"To set me up."

"Set you up? Like frame you?"

"Yes."

"Why would they want to do that?"

"Because I think they have been stealing from the company."

"How so?"

"I'm not entirely sure."

"Okay, what makes you believe that?"

"I work at the front desk. I accept payments, take reservations, and give guests their receipts. Do you recall when the city changed the way they disperse hospitality taxes to the county government?"

"I do."

This past summer, the City of Myrtle Beach sent out a memo alerting residents that they would no longer send hospitality taxes to the county and keep the fees within the city limits. The county started collecting those fees two decades ago. The city filed suit, stating that such collections were illegal. A judge agreed, and the city began collecting and keeping their own taxes.

The battle over the hospitality fees commenced earlier this year when the City of Myrtle Beach sued Horry County for continuing to collect hospitality fees within the municipalities, even though its right to do so ended a couple years ago.

Worry lines creased her brow. "After all that went into effect, I noticed something when people checked out."

"What's that?"

"I noticed that the tax rate was the same as it used to be.'

"Didn't the city lower the tax rate by half a percent or something when they started keeping the taxes for themselves?"

"Yes."

"Why were you all still charging the same rate?"

She shrugged. "Don't know."

As a business owner, I had to keep up with the taxes and tax rates. When the rate would change, I would have to go into our point-of-sale system and adjust the percentages. I figured that a resort would have to do something similar on their end when that occurred.

"Who would make that change?"

"Her name is Sabrina. She works in the cash office upstairs."

"Did you mention this to her or anyone else?"

She pursed her lips. "I did yesterday."

"To whom?"

"Mrs. Whitaker."

I blinked twice in rapid succession. She fidgeted.

My mind raced about what to ask next. The acid in my stomach churned. I realized that I hadn't eaten lunch yet. Could be that.

"What did she say?"

"Paige told us during orientation that she had an open-door policy. If we had questions or concerns to come to her and she would either handle it herself or run it up the ladder."

"How long had you suspected this?"

"A few months. At first, I thought Sabrina hadn't gotten around to changing it yet, but it came up in one of our staff meetings about the tax change and she sat there and said nothing."

"Have other coworkers noticed this?"

"Not that I'm aware of. Most are there to collect a paycheck. They don't care about the actual job."

"Do you?"

She held a hand to her chest. "I do. I love it. I find it exciting. People all over the world come to our resort. I come from a small

DEATH ON THE BOARDWALK

village in Moldova where everyone knows each other. Most are involved in the fishing trade. Here, guests come from all walks of life."

Put in that light, I wondered if Natasha coming to America was like Alice going through the looking glass. What might be normal to me was magical to her.

"I enjoy that about this job, too. Talking to and meeting customers." Getting back on topic, I said, "What did Paige say when you told her?"

"At first, she seemed to think it was a clerical error. Happens all the time, she said. Then I told her about the staff meeting and Sabrina not saying anything when the hospitality tax subject came up."

"What did she say then?"

"Said she would ask Sabrina about it."

"Did she?"

"I do not know. That was yesterday. I know Sabrina was at work, so I assumed she did."

"Seems like too important of a subject to let it simmer. It's theft."

"Yes, it is."

"Did any of your guests notice the tax variance?"

"No. Who would check the local tax rates before they come to stay?"

"Yeah, most people think little about the taxes on their receipts. They accept it and move on."

"Exactly."

"Then what happened?"

"Paige thanked me for the information and told me to keep it to myself since it was a subject sensitive to the business. I left her office and went home."

"And you think this led to Paige's death?"

A tear streamed from her eye down her cheek. "It's possible."

"Why do you think that?"

She swiped the back of her hand across her nose. "Because of Sabrina's boyfriend."

"What about her boyfriend?"

"He's not a good person."

"What makes you say that?"

"He also works for the resort."

That didn't exactly answer the question. "What does he do there?"

"He is in the upper management. He oversees the financial aspects or something. Travels a lot for the company."

"And his girlfriend happens to work for him?"

"Yes." She pronounced her Y's with a bit of J. More like, "Jess."

"Does the resort have any rules about coworkers dating?"

"They do among us hourly employees, but not with the ownership group."

"Oh, so he's one of the owners."

She nodded. "He has some minor ownership in the company, I think. Like, he handles finances, but doesn't do a lot with the business here in Myrtle Beach. Know what I mean?"

"I think. How did he become part-owner?"

"I do not know. It's been that way since I began working at OceanScapes."

"When was that?"

"Two years ago."

"What led you here?"

"I visited my older brother here in Myrtle Beach when he was here as a foreign exchange student. I was here for three months. So much more different than my country. He ended up staying. I returned when I came of age."

"Why did you come back?"

She gestured at the busy street. "So much more opportunity here than Moldova."

Understandable. "Are you here on a visa or something?"

"No, no," she said. "I am a citizen."

"What was it like to move here? Was it hard?"

"Not at all. There were many others from my area of the world here already. I found it easy to fit in."

Her appearance likely helped matters.

I tried to organize my thoughts aloud. "So, you noticed that OceanScapes still charged the guests the extra half percent and told Paige. Sabrina is the one who directly handles incoming money and her boyfriend is a part owner. And you haven't spoken to Sabrina about this?"

"No, I have not."

"Why?"

"Because of her boyfriend."

"Right, and what makes you think her boyfriend is not of good moral character?"

"Because he has been to jail before."

The hair on the back of my neck stood on end. "Oh really? Do you know why? What's his name?"

"I do not. His name is Chris McInally."

"Then how do you know about it?"

"Because my coworkers talk about it and him."

Gossip in the workplace is both dangerous and helpful. A

danger when spreading wrong information. Helpful if it uncovered a truth. "Besides Chris being an ex-con, is there a reason why he is a bad person?"

She looked to the side at the books on a shelf and considered her reply. "He always smiles at me. Specifically." I saw why, but didn't say this. "When he talks to me, his eyes don't stay on mine for long. They travel down to my shoes and back up to the locket around my neck."

A golden heart-shaped locket dangled from her neck, above her décolletage. I had the feeling that he wasn't studying the necklace.

"He has oily, greased back hair, like you'd see in the mafia movies. He never seems to be able to finish a sentence around me. Like he starts a thought and trails off."

"Does he talk like a mobster?" I was only half-joking.

"I think so, but again, I am not familiar enough with English accents to say either way."

"It sounds to me like this Chris is more creepy than bad."

"No, no. He is bad."

"He gives you that impression?"

"He reminds me of the many distrustful people in Moldova. You need to meet him. And Sabrina."

I sat up straight in my chair. "Me? Why me?"

"Because I think you can help." She studied me. "And there's something that makes me think you want to."

I had never spoken to this young woman before today, but she seemed like an excellent judge of character. She had me nailed. The fact was, I wanted to help for other reasons.

"What do you want me to do?"

"I have an idea."

CHAPTER
EIGHT

I showed Natasha out a few minutes later with a plan formed. It would have to wait until tomorrow.

Karen was ringing up a customer who had a tall stack of books sitting atop the counter. I didn't want to interrupt the transaction, so I headed to the coffee bar instead.

While I poured another cup of coffee, the patron thanked Karen, and walked out the door juggling her pocketbook, a bag of books, and an umbrella. Several other customers browsed through various areas of the store. Frank Sinatra crooned over the speakers.

"Gracious, Clark," Karen said from behind the counter. "I've already had to shoo away reporters from The Sun Times and Channel 7."

Karen was a great gatekeeper. She kept various vendors, insurance agents, and other nuisances out of my hair. My other employee, Margaret, was not so great in that regard.

"Thanks, Karen."

"Why were you in your office with that pretty girl from OceanScapes? Are you getting involved in this?"

"I'd rather not say why she was here, but I think I can connect some dots the police won't be able to see."

Her blue eyes scrutinized me for an extended beat. "Does it have to do with Autumn?"

The question hurt, but I had to admit that it had a ring of truth to it. Autumn was forty-one when she died. Two years older than me. Much too young. She had had an irregular heartbeat for her entire life and died of a sudden, massive heart attack while at work down at the courthouse late one evening.

We had been married for fifteen years and had not conceived any children. We had entered a fertilization study conducted by Yale University through a local hospital. After running through a gamut of tests, they gave me a vitamin with a mix of antioxidants to take for three months. Researchers believed the pill would improve the chances of conception.

A pregnancy test proved positive after one month. We were joyous. She died two weeks later.

I've been a bit of a mess since then. I focused on my business, writing, and helping others, finding that the less free time I had, the better. Kept my mind off of what happened. Her death taught me the value of life. No more taking risks. No more taking chances. Life can be taken away at any moment. I was determined to live a long, long time, always keeping her in my heart.

Not wanting to answer Karen's question, I asked, "Ready for lunch? I'll spell you for a while."

She put her hands on her hips. "You sure?"

"I'm sure. Go. Eat. Enjoy." I laughed and waved a hand at the store. "Besides, it's not like it's busy right now."

"'Okay. Thanks." She beamed. "I have this new Margaret Mitchell book I'm itching to get into."

She reached under the counter, grabbed her pocketbook and

book, and left the store. I figured she was headed a few blocks down to the 2nd Avenue Pier. That's where she usually went for her lunches. She liked to get a bite from the restaurant there, walk out on the pier, and eat and read.

A half hour passed with quiet in the store when Erica from WMHF walked in with a smile on her face meant to butter me up.

It doesn't stop.

"Hi Clark. I'm back."

"I can see that." I stepped out to greet her. "Care to sit down at a table?"

"No, no. I'll stand."

I looked behind her. "No cameraman?"

"Chuck? No, he's in the truck. I'll call him in if I feel like I need him. This doesn't have to be on camera. In my report, I'll say that a witness told me yadda, yadda, yadda."

I cocked my head to one side. "Wait. Was that a Seinfeld reference?"

She laughed. "Yup. You got me. Love that show."

I figured Miss Sullivan here would be in her mid-twenties and not a child of the nineties when that show was popular. Interesting that she would be a fan. "Me too. But thanks, that's a relief."

"Yeah. Most people in your situation don't want to be on camera. Anyway, cat's out of the bag," she said referring to the police statement on the death of Paige. "Can you talk now?"

"I can." Not that I wanted to.

Another electric smile. "Great." She took out her phone and tapped the screen a few times. "Mind if I record this?"

"Be my guest."

"Great," she echoed. "Can you tell me what happened this morning, from your point of view?"

I laid out the course of events as best I could. It was almost the same statement I gave to Gomez this morning.

"So," Erica said and pointed to the rear of the store. "There was a body laying back there?"

"That's right. My employee said that the victim was in here yesterday buying books to take on a vacation that was supposed to start today."

Her bottom lip puckered out. "That's sad. I wonder if she needed to stop by her work this morning for something before going?"

"That would be my guess." I didn't need to raise any theories about why a quick visit to OceanScapes would have resulted in her death. Perhaps Erica would, though. "Can I ask you a question?"

She straightened. This reporter probably wasn't used to having the tables turned by her interviewee. "Have you been digging into this all day?"

"I have. News is slow this time of year. A random murder is big for us."

"Detective Gomez said on the news that they were pursuing a few leads. Do you know anything about that?"

"No. Not specifically."

"Do you have any suspicions?"

"Hmm, not any suspicions, per se. Some inklings, perhaps."

"What kind of inklings?"

"I went down to OceanScapes and spoke to a few of the employees."

Thinking of Natasha, I said, "Yeah, we've had a few come in

here. Guess they called everyone in to break the news. At least, that's what I was told."

"That's not necessarily true," she said. "Mind if we sit now?"

The bell above the front door jingled. Karen was back. I wanted to hear what Erica learned at OceanScapes.

"Yeah," I said. Karen and I made eye contact. She knew what she needed to do. She nodded and walked behind the counter, stowing her purse and the thick book underneath.

I led Erica over to the same table Detective Gomez and I sat at this morning. "Cup of coffee?"

"No thanks. None for me. Do you have tea?"

"I do. Earl Grey fine?"

"Absolutely. My favorite."

After a few minutes, I placed a steaming mug in front of her. The string from a tea bag swayed over the lip. "Thanks."

"You're welcome. Fresh from the Charleston Tea Plantation."

"Ooo."

I settled in across from her. "So, if they didn't call all the employees down there to tell them about Paige, why were they there?"

"Well, telling them about Paige was one reason. The other was for the police to question them."

That kept Gomez and Moody busy. "Someone told me that there are thirty or so employees. A lot to dig through."

"Yeah, glad I didn't have to do it. There was a horde of police there. From the city and county."

"I'm sure."

"What did the employees you spoke with say?"

"Some were astonished and saddened. Mrs. Whitaker seemed universally loved."

"What about those who weren't astonished or saddened?"

"That's where it got interesting."

"How so?"

"It seems that there's been some friction of late with Paige and upper management."

"Oh. Why?"

"That's what no one could figure out."

"Then how do they know there is any discord to begin with?"

She puckered her lips and narrowed her brow before responding. "I think they could tell; you know. Like, the ones who had been there for a long time saw Paige interact with the directors, managers, and ownership group and noticed something changed."

"Recently?"

"I think so." She pulled the string from the tea bag and bobbed it up and down a few times. I set a spoon and a rectangular dish containing various packets of sweeteners in front of her. She ignored them and instead picked up the mug and took a sip. She winced from the heat, but recovered. "From what I could gather, no one seemed to be able to pinpoint when this change began."

If Natasha told Paige about the hospitality tax discrepancy yesterday, then whatever her beef was with the higher ups was something different. Something unrelated.

"Did anyone mention any names?"

"To me? No, I'm just a reporter. I could only speak to a couple of them before getting run out of the building."

"They gave you the boot?"

"Yeah, part of the job." A thin smile crept across her face. "I think the ones who told me about the tension didn't want it connecting back to them. If word got out that Joe Executive had gotten into it with Paige, then someone like Joe Executive could trace that argument back to the informant, since the staff in that place is so small."

"Job security. Isn't their office across the street from the actual hotel?"

"Yeah, you check in on one side of Ocean Boulevard and then go back across to your room and amenities. And the offices are on two levels behind the check-in desk."

"Do you know where Paige's office was? First or second story?"

"I'm not sure. Never thought to ask."

"Do you know if they think she was killed there? At OceanScapes?"

"Oh yes. They had everything taped off. Saw forensics going in and out. I couldn't get back there." She crossed her arms. "Wait, why are you asking me questions?"

I didn't want to reveal anything about my past to her, so I said, "Common human interest."

She narrowed her eyes. I hoped that the reporter in her wouldn't keep digging.

"If you say so," she said. "Look, I have a feeling you have a little more than 'common human interest' going on here. I'm not going to push you. Tell you what, let's stay in touch. You seem like a snoop. Or at least someone who keeps their antenna up. If you hear or stumble across anything, how about letting me know?"

I thought about what my new friend Natasha suspected. And then there was Gomez. She seemed at least open with me. I didn't think she was withholding any information when we were together. It was like I was holding the strings of three balloons floating around independently of each other. If I could hold them together without them bumping into each other too much, I might learn things that none of them could by themselves.

"I'll do that," I said, "only if you do the same for me."

She rocked back and forth in her chair for a moment before sticking out her hand. "Deal."

I shook it and showed her to the door. There wasn't much to say after that.

CHAPTER
NINE

The Myrtle Beach City Services building sat on Oak Street, within walking distance of Myrtle Beach Reads. I drove, forgoing the exercise. As usual. The sun had set. It would be fully dark by the time this meeting of the Downtown Development Corporation ended.

The group exists to help revitalize Myrtle Beach's central business district. With nearly twenty million annual visitors to Myrtle Beach, it was important to add reasons and appeal to keep them coming back—and bringing their friends and extended families. Moves made by the group brought in new business and investors. A new Arts and Innovation District was in the works.

All of this was helpful to my business. I didn't have a named role with the group, but I attended most meetings, and, for some reason, other business owners and investors took an interest in my opinions.

The meetings took place in a conference room deep within the bowels of the government building, surrounded by wood panel walls straight out of the 1980s. The shell of the room was in stark contrast to the modern, glass-topped conference table with eighteen seats taking up most of the space. A long table with finger foods and beverages nestled against one wall. A computer hooked up to a projector ran by a technician with curly brown hair sat at one end of the table.

A louder than normal buzz from this gathering greeted me as I snuck in right as the meeting came to order. I arrived late because I knew what the primary topic of conversation would be as the attendees gathered: Paige's death and me finding the body.

I hoped to make a break for it as soon as this meeting adjourned. Skipping this was not an option as there were several important topics on the agenda. One purpose of this meeting was to give an update on the progress of the Arts and Innovation District. Now that that was moving along, one of their other initiatives was on the Boardwalk.

There weren't any set seats except for those with roles in the Corporation. I sat midway down one side, facing the refreshments table. The projector screen was to my left. To my right was one of my favorite business owners in this circle, Marilyn. I searched her out when I entered the room and she had reserved a spot for me to her left.

Her hair was green and tied off in pigtails. It was blue the last time I saw her. Red the time before that. I'm surprised her hair didn't fall out from all the chemical treatments. Autumn always kept to her natural red hair. Didn't need to mess with perfection.

I couldn't count the number of piercings Marilyn had, nor would I want to. She dressed mostly in black all the time, from head to combat-booted toe. She threw in a splash of color today with a Cheshire Cat t-shirt. A definite misfit in this mostly strait-laced group.

You might ask yourself why she was my favorite of the group. Part of the answer is her unique sense of humor, and she kept the others in these gatherings on their toes. I admired that. She didn't care what others thought of her, as shown by her appearance. Marilyn was the youngest person here by ten years, at least, but one of the brightest.

She didn't look like she belonged. But you can't judge a book by its cover.

Several gathered around the table had eyes on me as I situated myself in the seat. I saw Theresa around the way. We made eye contact. She blew me a kiss. My cheeks warmed, and I looked away. The smell of stale coffee lingered in the room like it had infused itself in the woodgrain walls. A paper on the table in front of me held the evening's agenda.

As I glanced over it, Marilyn leaned towards me and whispered, "Geez Clark. Way to keep a low profile."

"Thanks," I returned. "Keeping my head down is my specialty."

"Right." She placed a hand on my right arm. "I heard about what happened, man. I'm so sorry."

"Thanks, but I feel sorrier for Paige."

She withdrew her hand, properly admonished. "Yes, of course."

"I'm sorry. I didn't mean to be harsh."

"No, no. No worries. Yes, it's horrible what happened. I feel so sorry for her."

"Did you know her?"

"I didn't. I knew of her. A lot of their younger employees frequent the shop."

Marilyn's comic book shop in the middle of the Boardwalk

was called We Have Issues. She opened a few years ago and is immensely popular during the summer months. We didn't directly compete, thankfully. I didn't stock too many comic books in my store to begin with. It didn't take long after I opened that those sales went away and I stopped carrying them.

We Have Issues sits between a candy store and The Gay Dolphin Gift Cove. One struggle Downtown Myrtle Beach businesses have during the off months is attracting customers. While Myrtle Beach Reads has books for all ages, We Have Issues has more of a niche offering to a shorter segment of the population. It so happens that segment is highly enthusiastic about the stories of the superheroes and villains lining the racks of Marilyn's store, but they are more of a summer crowd. Marilyn organizes several Comic Book Conventions (Comicons) throughout the offseason at the Myrtle Beach Convention Center and other gathering spots in the area. That keeps her money flowing during the offseason.

There is still a local working population year-round. Many of the jobs in downtown are held by younger people.

"Have any of them been in today? OceanScapes people?" I asked.

"A few this morning and this afternoon. The ones from earlier said the higher ups summoned them but didn't know why. The afternoon crowd was much more morose."

"They'd probably found out by then."

"Yeah. They learned the news before it came out to the public after lunch."

"A few came in this morning. I accidentally broke the news to them."

"Who was it you told?"

"Gloria and Natasha."

"I'm not familiar with them."

"As I'm sure you have customers from OceanScapes I don't know, either."

"Touché. I'm sure they were surprised when you told them."

"Absolutely. Gloria had to sit down. She and Paige were close."

"I bet. Man, I can't imagine. How did the other woman take it?"

I paused before answering. "She was better about it. She's from one of those Eastern European countries where she probably had a rougher upbringing than you or I. She seems like she has a thick skin. Did you speak to any of the employees?"

"I did. I was by myself for most of the day. Bored. Wasn't much business, so I had to keep myself entertained."

"Any of them say anything to you?"

"About what?"

"Paige's death," I said. That should be obvious.

"Well yeah, dummy. What else was there to talk about?"

I didn't answer her rhetorical question. "What did they say?"

"They were surprised. Couldn't have happened to a nicer person. She was their first point of contact when they interviewed for their jobs, so she left some sort of impression on all of them."

And one of them may have killed her. "Anyone say why they thought she was killed?"

"What are you? A cop?"

"That's the second time someone has asked me that today.

No, just interested in why her body was sitting on my doorstep this morning."

She patted my arm again. "Sorry, man."

A vision of peeling back the rug and finding Paige in it leaped into my mind.

"To answer your question though," Marilyn said, "one kid said that he heard Paige arguing with someone in her office while he was punching the time clock. It apparently got pretty heated."

I leaned forward and put my elbows on the table. "Did he see who she was arguing with?"

"He didn't say, but then again, I didn't ask."

"Did he say when this was?"

"Yesterday, actually."

"Who was it you spoke with?"

"He's a young black kid. Solomon. Loves his Incredible Hulk."

I took a mental note of his name. "Let me know if you see him again."

"You want to talk to him?"

"Maybe."

A line appeared between her brows. "Let the cops handle this, Clark."

"Come on," I pleaded.

"Okay, I will. But don't go poking your cute nose in places it's not supposed to be and stay out of trouble."

I held up a hand, crossing my thumb over a curled pinky. "Scout's honor."

The corner of her mouth quirked up. "You dope."

Someone at the head of the table cleared their throat. The

mayor of Myrtle Beach, Sid Rosen, stood there. His blue eyes landing on everyone who was seated, like a strict schoolteacher. He had a charismatic aura about him. The type that made people take notice when he walked into a room.

"If you will all give me your attention, this meeting will begin in two minutes. We'll wait and see if we have any stragglers coming in late."

Everyone either straightened out whatever papers or folder they had before them, silenced phones, clicked pens, or took a sip of whatever beverage they had. Someone went to the open double door and started closing it when one more person shuffled through.

He was about average height, but stout like a bodybuilder, and had slicked back dark hair. The sleeves were rolled back on his dress shirt, revealing barbwire tattoos wrapped around both forearms. He grabbed the only vacant seat remaining at the table, directly across from me. He placed his briefcase on the floor before sitting.

It was the first time I had seen him here.

He settled in and ran a hand through his hair. I hoped he had a handkerchief or something to wipe his hands on afterward. He had a high hair to hair grease ratio.

Marilyn purred next to me. The other women at the table were either looking directly at him or trying to hide the fact that the stranger intrigued them.

An OceanScapes logo was embroidered above the shirt pocket on the left side of his shirt. His eyes seemed to search for mine. I knew why. He fit the description that Natasha gave me earlier of Sabrina's boyfriend, Chris. A minority owner of the resort and in charge of finance — which explained why he would join this group.

It didn't explain why this was his first time coming. Normally their vice president, Martin Something-Or-Other, attended these meetings. Maybe he had sent Chris in his place.

The man across from me had keen eyes boring into mine that reflected reptilian intelligence.

Like a snake.

The meeting moved along at a snail's pace. Various board members stumped for their various agendas. The hospitality taxes got pushed off until next year. No one could decide on what should be done with the newfound income stream. Then we came to the security cameras along the Boardwalk.

There was disagreement between board members about installing cameras on a secondary, less-trafficked street. Doing that would blow through a large part of the budget reserved for other projects. A budget that would be bolstered with the increase in funding from the hospitality taxes. A few of those were pet projects important to one or two on the board which, if done, would help their bottom line.

I raised a finger and caught the mayor's eye.

"Yes, Mr. Thomas. Do you have something to add?"

"I do," I said. "I'm sure by now everyone knows what happened this morning."

"Yes, very tragic," the mayor said. Others murmured their agreement.

I made eye contact with Snake Eyes, er, Chris. "We're sorry for your loss."

"Thank you," he said. "It's been a tough day for all of us. Paige was a big part of OceanScapes and had been with us since the beginning. Her loss leaves a big hole, not just in position, but in the overall morale of the resort."

Then sat back and grew silent. That's all? Sounded rehearsed. I liked his Scottish brogue, though.

I continued. "The problem the police have is that there are no cameras on that section of Flagg Street. I have a camera feed from above the door, but it's a very narrow view. Not much better than looking through a peephole."

"Did they find footage from anywhere between OceanScapes and your store?" someone asked.

"Not that I'm aware of," I said. "Then again, I'm not exactly privy to everything they know. I gave them my part of the story. Had cameras been there, they probably could have already found the killer, or at least know who it is. We should get those cameras installed so this doesn't happen again."

"It's a small price to pay to keep anyone else from getting killed," Marilyn said. "Don't you believe it would help cut down on other crimes too?"

"Probably would have kept those hoodlums from stealing my merch from the back of my store," said Earl. He owned a t-shirt airbrushing shop in the main drag of the Boardwalk. He spoke with a gruff voice and Long Island accent.

"Yeah, I might not have been vandalized last summer too," Sharon, the owner of a hot dog stand near my store, added.

Marilyn held a hand down beside her chair under the table. I reached down and gave her a low five. We'd thrown chum in the water and whipped the sharks into a frenzy. By the end of the meeting, a plan was in place to get the camera project moving. Since the legwork on estimates and prices were already done, all someone had to do was call the installers.

But for Paige, it was too little, too late.

The meeting adjourned. I was gathering my things when the mayor tapped my shoulder. I noticed that Chris had already bid a hasty retreat from the room.

"Mr. Mayor. Good evening." We shook hands.

"Mr. Thomas," he returned. "I'd say the same to you, but I have the feeling that your evening hasn't been, eh, pleasant?"

"It was better than this morning."

"I'm sure. They briefed me on what happened to Paige."

"What did happen to Paige? Did they tell you that? Gomez said on the news that they had some leads."

He shook his head. "No, not really. They say that to comfort the public. I'm not sure that they have any suspects yet."

Interesting. "Did they have cameras down at OceanScapes?"

"They do, but there's a problem with them."

"Let me guess, the cameras don't work?"

"No, they work. Whoever did this spray painted over the lenses before they killed Paige."

"What? You're joking."

"I'm not. That's what they told me."

My mind whirred. Her murder had to have been premeditated. Several meeting attendees left. A few others lagged behind, speaking in small groups.

"Anyway, how are you? I know the strain you had to be under when Autumn died. This had to bring a lot of that back."

"It does." Thanks for reminding me, I thought. Probably not something proper to say aloud to the mayor. Perhaps he could read my mind and get my reaction.

He caught the change in my demeanor and placed a hand on my shoulder. "Hang in there," he said and walked off to speak to someone else.

My interactions with Mayor Rosen were always brief. He was a busy man. The conversations seemed shorter after Autumn's passing.

I collected my things and drove home pondering the spray painted cameras. Was the spray paint brought from home or did OceanScapes have a supply of it somewhere?

CHAPTER
TEN

Crashing waves of an early morning high tide pushed dense fog on shore, draping the Boardwalk in a thick white blanket.

Yesterday, Natasha told me to meet her down at OceanScapes around ten. I was brewing two urns of coffee when Margaret came over to the coffee bar.

She had to come around the side in order to speak to me. She wasn't tall enough to see over the counter. Silver-rimmed glasses accented her dark skin. Thick lenses magnified her eyes. Gray hair fell to her shoulders.

The older, retired former librarian had a love of books that was unmatched. When she interviewed for the job, we thought Margaret was too old. At first glance, she looked like she had one foot in the grave. Her shoulders stooped. You could hear her labored breathing from across a crowded room. There was no way she could handle the workload.

At sixty-five, the county library forced Margaret to retire. They said she could not handle her position as head librarian anymore, and she had to either take a demotion or retire. Margaret believed that they pressured her because there was another, much younger, female librarian who sought after Margaret's position. This "young tart"—as Margaret put it—

was having a fling with the county commissioner.

I never imagined there was such politicking at the local library.

That occurred eight years ago. No matter how she arrived in my life, I was glad Margaret was here. Partly because of her diligent, organized work, the store was a success.

"Clark, what are you doing?" Margaret said in a tone that reminded me of my mother's when she caught me misbehaving. I had already related yesterday's events to her before the store opened.

"I'm going to take some coffee down to OceanScapes for them."

"And why are you doing that?"

"Yesterday, one of their workers commented on how poor the quality of the coffee in their break room is. I thought I'd do my part to make their day a little better."

"Sure," she said, tapping her foot. "I don't believe that nonsense for a second."

There was no fooling Margaret or Karen. They kept me in line. "What do you want me to say, Margaret?"

"That you're going there to poke around."

I lifted my hands in mock surrender. "Alright. Guilty as charged."

"This isn't like you, Clark."

"Like what?"

"Jumping headfirst into this. I talked to Karen last night. She filled me in on what you were up to. You don't do anything without a plan." She drummed a finger against her chin. "I don't understand why you feel the need to go poking your nose in business that doesn't concern you."

"It does in a way. I want to find out why someone would kill her and dump her body at my business. Did it have something to do with me?"

"That's the police's job. Besides, what if you get hot on the trail of someone and they decide they're going to do to you what they did to Paige?" Her question brought me up short. "What kind of self-defense training do you have?"

"None," I admitted.

She poked a finger at my belly. "That's reason alone why you should back off and stay in your lane."

She had a point, besides the one at the end of the finger jabbing in my midsection. "I don't know what to tell you, Margaret. I feel like I need to do something."

"Promise me you'll be careful."

"I will."

"Okay. Then go on with yourself."

After filling the carafes, I grabbed them by the handles, toted them out the door and started toward OceanScapes. The resort was a couple blocks down the strip. The fog had burned off and given way to sunny skies.

Green waves crashed on shore as the tide reached its height. The stationary SkyWheel poked above the buildings behind me. Several people wearing light jackets passed into view along the shore, scanning the beach for shells. This was one of the better areas in Myrtle Beach for beach combing.

It was a sad day for some, but would be a happy day for others later. The first of the departing visitors at the Wayfarer Motel were loading luggage into their vehicles.

Outside of the resort motels, there were mostly small businesses in this section of Myrtle Beach. We all knew one another and worked together to provide tourists with a memorable experience that kept them coming back. Many people who worked on the Boardwalk came into the shop. I've come to know them well over the years.

Millions of visitors came through Myrtle Beach every year. But somehow, seeing many of the same local faces often lent a small-town vibe.

Wednesdays were a transition day in Myrtle Beach this time of year. Most people came on the weekends. The visitors coming this weekend were at home packing. They would start arriving on Thursday and then come in earnest on Friday.

That's why Wednesdays were one of my favorite days. This is when I got my paperwork and payroll done and bury myself in my office and work on whatever novel my ghostwriting gig had provided me.

Today was obviously different.

The OceanScapes tower came into view and grew as I kept walking. It rose above the other resorts nearby. Blue bricks in a wavy pattern bisected the tall, white structure. Azure windows lined either side. Its midsection was a collage of vertical lines and circles. The architect who designed the building must have thought it would look as good underwater as it does above. It stood out in a crowd of Myrtle Beach resorts designed to catch the eye.

While the hotel and amenities were on the ocean side of the street, check-in and the offices sat in a miniaturized version on the other side.

Palm fronds whipped in the salty breeze on the far side of the parking lot. The fog was burning off. Soft rays of morning sunlight cascaded over the waves and cast the tall oceanfront tower in shades of orange and pink. A tang of salt clung to the air.

I walked up the steps and entered a plain lobby compared to the lofty structure across the street where guests stayed. Natasha and another man were at the desk attending to travelers, checking out with slouched shoulders and languid expressions. Can't blame them. I wouldn't be happy about going home either.

The other guy finished first and greeted me with a smile. He looked college-aged, wore a gray suit, and had black, spiked hair in the front.

"Good morning," he said. "How can I help you today?"

I raised both coffee urns and before I could speak, Natasha turned to the guy and said, "Hey Ray, can you finish with these guests for me? I'll handle him."

Ray gave me a quick glance, perhaps glad that he didn't have to talk to the crazy guy carrying two jugs of coffee. "Sure thing, Natasha."

Natasha apologized to the couple in front of her but told them they were in the capable hands of Ray.

"Good morning," she said after stepping around the desk. "You're right on time. I wish I told you to come a little later. Ten a.m. is check-out time."

"Oh, I'm sorry. Want me to come back?"

"No, no. It's okay." She looked back at Ray as their shared guests were leaving the now empty lobby. "Ray, I'm going to take him back to the break room. Yell if you need me."

He held a hand up. "Not a problem."

"Thanks," she said.

She slid a keycard through a slot in a door hidden from my

view in the lobby before entering a restricted area. We traveled down a hallway lined with various labor laws, notices, workplace policies, employee of the month posters and information boards along with framed photos fit for advertising brochures. We passed one man with his head down, eyes intent on a sheaf of papers.

"That's Martin," she whispered. "He's the vice-president of OceanScapes."

"Yeah, I've met him before at a couple city meetings."

We arrived at the break room and paused outside the door.

"Both of them are here," she said.

"Chris and Sabrina?"

She nodded. "They sealed the executive offices and they allow anyone but the police up there. I have not spoken to either of them. The execs took over the conference room," she pointed past me, "down there. I saw Sabrina earlier, and she gave me a dirty look. Or maybe I was imagining it."

"Could have," I said. "Everyone is probably tense around here."

"Yes." She peered through the doorway into the break room. "Neither are in there."

She gave me a good description of Chris last evening but didn't say much about Sabrina's appearance. "What does Sabrina look like?"

She pursed her lips. "She's tall, like you." She expanded her arms at her hips. "Big and has short brown hair. Bulging eyes. You'll know her when you see her."

"Okay."

"It looks like there are five executives at the same table and some other workers scattered around the room." This plan of hers was only half-formed. She fiddled with a keycard in one hand and shifted from leg to leg. "Please, see what you can find out."

I wasn't sure what I could learn, nor what I would do with any information. However, I can't turn down a request for help.

"Excuse me," a man wearing a gray custodial outfit said as he pressed between us carrying a full bag of trash.

We parted so he could step past. "Sorry, James," Natasha said.

He touched the bill of his hat. "No problem, ma'am."

Sunlight streamed in as he opened an exit door a short distance away and walked through, keys on a ring attached to his belt jingling all the way.

"James is one of the leaders on our maintenance staff. Might be a good idea to speak with him. He's everywhere. He could probably give you some gossip, at least."

"Noted."

Natasha led me into the room and pointed at a table against the wall. It was piled with boxes of donuts, a platter of cold-cut sandwiches, and several jugs of sweet teas and lemonades with varying levels of fullness.

A somber mood greeted us. Several people looked up from their phones or hushed conversations.

As I placed the urns on the counter and twisted the tops to allow pouring, Natasha introduced me to a group of people clustered at a table near the rear of the room.

"This is Clark. He owns the bookstore up the street."

Three of them looked at me with placid eyes and expressionless faces. The others put two and two together.

"Wait," one woman with curly dark hair drawled. "Are you

the poor fella who found Paige?"

"I am."

Her hand shot up to her face. "Oh, my goodness sakes. That's terrible. I felt so bad for you."

What about feeling sorry for Paige? I almost responded. "Thank you."

"I'm Linda."

"Nice to meet you," I said. "I wish it could have been under better circumstances."

"Ain't that the truth," Linda said.

Natasha jumped in. "Clark knew things would be chaotic down here, and I mentioned to him one time how bad our coffee is here in the break room."

"Preach it, sister," a woman at another table added.

Natasha raised a fist in solidarity and continued. "Anyway, he brought us some of his wonderful coffee."

"I've had his before," an older gentleman at the table in front of us said. He looked vaguely familiar with his thinning gray hair and hawkish nose.

"Thanks," I said.

Natasha reached down into a cabinet and withdrew a stack of paper cups. She placed them on the table beside the coffee before gathering containers of sugar and creamer.

No wonder she said no one liked their coffee. I had a great disdain for powdered creamer. To me, it tasted fake and unnatural and left a filmy feeling on my tongue. Might as well be dusted chalk. I should have brought some half and half.

"Grab a cup and join us," Linda said to me.

I wondered how I would join in the conversation and spent last night and this morning trying to visualize ways to get involved. That wasn't discussed in our half-baked scheme. This solved my dilemma.

I made a show of checking my watch, even though Margaret could hold down the fort for an extended period by herself. "Sure thing."

After grabbing a cup of coffee, black, I sat at a proffered chair near the middle of the break room. Natasha made eye contact with me and nodded her head toward the front desk. She had to get back to work.

"Thanks for showing me back here, ma'am," I said.

"You're welcome," Natasha said and left the room.

The hand I held the cup in shook, causing the coffee to slosh around inside. Steady, I told myself, relieved that I only poured half a cup. Standing in a room full of strangers wasn't my forte. The chair was still warm.

Linda pointed at everyone in the room and introduced them by name.

"Nice to meet you all," I said. "I'm horrible with names when I first meet people, so it's great that most of you are wearing a name badge."

"Clark? Is that your first or last name?" Linda asked me.

"Middle name, actually. My first name is Beauregard."

"Why do you go by Clark?"

"Uh, because my parents named me after a Muppet."

"A Muppet?" several said in unison.

It's a story I've repeated many times in my life. "Yes, somewhere around the time I was born, Jim Henson added a new character to The Muppet Show named Beauregard. She loved him so much that they named me after him."

A few people giggled.

"I think I remember him," Linda said. "Wasn't he a bit of a dimwit?"

"Yeah, once I was old enough to figure it out, I started going by my middle name. Mom threw a fit when she learned that I requested to go by that moniker at school. She understood once I explained myself."

"That's cute," a surly woman with a mullet said. She sounded like she smoked five packs a day.

"Yeah, that's my mom. Look, I'm sorry for what happened to Paige," I said to the gathered employees.

"Why are you sorry?" said a man to my right. His name tag identified him as Terry. He patted me on the shoulder. "You had nothing to do with it. There's nothing to be sorry for."

"Thanks, man. I'm not sure what to say in these situations."

"None of us are, honey," a woman, Tanzee, at the executive table said. "It's a sad, sad day around here."

"That it is," someone else agreed. Murmurs of assent echoed around the room.

"Can you tell us about what happened on your end?" Linda said.

"Sure," I said, filling them in on the details. I left nothing out in case someone might pick up on something. Some moaned. Some shook their heads in disgust. Losing Paige was an enormous loss for OceanScapes, not just job wise, but in the morale department too. After ending my story, I said, "I'm sure her death has been the big topic of conversation around here this morning."

"The only topic," someone said.

I took a sip of the coffee and tilted my head forward. "Why would anyone do this?"

Several people exchanged looks. They suspected something. Except for the ones at their exclusive table. Their expressions were unchanged. Hmm. Might be more difficult to extract information with the blue-collar workers and white-collar workers mixed here.

"I know those drilling groups gave her a hard time a couple years ago," Terry said. "Maybe they still have a sour taste in their mouths and wanted revenge."

"Like they set up a hit on her?" I said.

"Yeah, something like that."

"I'd heard that she didn't keep regular hours, and she was supposed to have been going on vacation. How would anyone know when she was alone in her office?"

"Oh, she liked to come in very early to get her paperwork done," Linda said. "Although she typically did that on Wednesdays, not Tuesdays like yesterday."

"What would she have been doing here?"

"It's a pay week," Tanzee said. "She was probably doing the payroll before she went on vacation so everyone could get paid this week."

One of the executives, Matt, spoke. "That's what it appeared to me that she was doing. A woman on our maintenance staff was the first to check her office after we found out about her death. She said she saw timecards scattered around the room. She could tell there was a scuffle."

That's what Natasha suggested. "Did I hear this right? That someone painted over the security cameras?"

Matt grimaced. "Where did you hear that?"

"From one of the higher ups in the city," I answered. I wasn't about to tell them that the mayor was my source.

The non-executives shared looks. This was news to them.

"Sounds like something an assassin would do," Terry said.

Others shared their agreement. That's how wild rumors start. Someone suggests something believable on some level and it takes off. It spreads on social media like wildfire. That's one reason I stay off those sites. People will believe anything they see or hear and don't question the source.

Not that I'm questioning Terry's suggestion. Who knows at this point?

"I bet those oil companies have deep enough pockets to hire someone to do that," Linda suggested.

Not wanting to continue that line of reasoning, I went back to the cameras, directing my question to Matt. "Were all of them painted?"

"No, not all. Just two. One outside the back door and one in the stairwell leading up to the offices. Hers was at the first office at the top of the stairs."

"Are there any cameras in the hallways?"

"No. You had to have a keycard to get in there. We know who has access to those offices."

"And they wouldn't have access unless they were of a certain position?"

"Gotcha." That narrowed down the suspect list.

Someone stuck their head in the door and got everyone's attention.

"Hey everyone," she directed at the executive table. "We're clear to go back up."

"The police are gone?" Tanzee asked.

"Yup. Can't get into Paige's office yet, though."

Judging from the somber looks at the power table, I

presumed no one was in a hurry to get into their late coworker's personal space anyway. One by one, the five higher-ups drained their coffee, collected their things and stood.

"Thanks for the coffee," Linda said. "I'm going to get up to your store soon."

"Yeah, I'll be there soon too. You wouldn't happen to sell any Margaret Atwood books, would you?" Tanzee asked.

"Have them all," I said. "One of my workers, Karen, is a big fan of hers. If you like Atwood, there're others she could suggest to you too."

Her mouth puckered into a crooked O. "Hmm, might have to take you up on that."

The five power players filed out of the room, eager to get back to their familiar territory. Didn't want to mingle with the common folks for any longer than needed.

That left three remaining. Terry and two women huddled together in a corner, eyes intent on their phones.

"Man, it's all messed up," Terry said to me after our corner of the room cleared.

"Yeah, it is," I agreed. "A death like this happens so fast that it makes you numb."

"No, no. That's not what I'm talking about. I mean, it is in a sense. But it's pretty messed up about them sitting here and acting like no one knows anything."

Terry had a shaved head, thin goatee, and a diamond stud in his left ear. A light blue dress shirt that looked two sizes too small, showed off bulging muscles underneath. He had a deep, slightly intimidating voice.

"What do you mean?"

"Let me give you the skinny. This is the first time I can

remember any of the execs sitting in this break room. They lock themselves upstairs," he pointed a finger at the ceiling, "and only come down to our level when they're summoned by guest complaints or to make sure we're doing our jobs correctly."

"How often does that happen?"

"Coupla times a day. See, we don't really know what they're doing up there. The only time we set foot in their chambers is when we clock in and out or are summoned to Paige's office for something." He looked away for a moment, trying to compose himself. I took a sip of coffee, savoring the richness. He came back. "But we don't know what's going on. We only hear rumors. No one knows where this company is going."

"Why's that?"

He leaned closer. "We've seen some strangers walking around with our owner, VP, and finance guy. Like they're inspecting the property."

"Oh, you think they're going to sell?"

"That's the hot rumor. The owner, Mr. Curtis—"

"I know him." He stared a dart at me when I interrupted him. I wouldn't do that again. The man definitely had an intimidation factor. "Sorry."

"We figure that because Curtis is getting up there in years, he might look to sell."

"Is there a succession plan for when he retires or passes?"

"That's just it. We don't know. They keep us in the dark on matters of business like that. Sure, they tell us when we're making, or not making, numbers. Good for us to know the bottom line, but as far as knowing what's going on with the way they're running the biz? We're clueless down here."

"Ignorance can be bliss."

He snorted and crossed his arms. "Not when our jobs could be in jeopardy. Let's say these people buy the place, come in, and change everything. Maybe they decide my job is no longer needed and give me the boot. Then what am I supposed to do?"

"I hear ya. It's tough when you depend on others for your livelihood."

"Yeah, but you own your own business." He pointed a finger at my chest. "You're one of them."

"True, but I wasn't born with a silver spoon in my mouth. My wife and I scraped to start this business. We had to put a lot of stuff on credit cards back in the early days. Remember, I have employees who depend on me too. If it came down to it, I'd pay them before I'd pay myself. That's the silent vow I made when I hired them."

He sat back in his chair and uncrossed his arms.

"What is your job here?" I said.

"I'm over guest experience in the pool area across the street."

"Seems like it's important."

"Not really, to be honest. I have to make sure the towels around the pool get picked up and cleaned and no one is getting drunk in there. I mean, they could replace me with a couple teenagers."

"Then why do you do it?"

"The money is pretty good, and I get to hang out by the ocean every day. Not a bad life."

No argument from me on that. "So, what do you think they know?"

"Who mighta killed her." He leaned in and spoke in a lower tone. "I've heard that she was pushing back against them selling. Something about the people wanting to buy the place that she didn't like."

"Why would they kill her over that?"

"Dunno. You'd have to find out what her beef was with the buyers."

As I wondered how I would go about doing that, he looked at his watch and downed the rest of his coffee in one gulp. "Look man, nice talking to you, but I gotta get back to it, you know?"

I shook his hand. "Nice talking to you, too. Don't be a stranger. Come up and see us."

"You have coffee like this every day?"

I nodded. "Every day."

"Cool, man. I'll be there. See ya."

He stood and walked out of the break room, tossing his cup in the trashcan on the way out. The two women in the corner laughed about something they saw on one phone. As I got to my feet to leave, a woman who had to be Sabrina walked in. She was not happy.

CHAPTER
ELEVEN

When I was a little kid, we didn't have cable. Rabbit ears only picked up a few stations, so it limited our viewing choices. I liked to watch cartoons like Transformers, the Smurfs, Bugs Bunny, Rocky and Bullwinkle, Yogi Bear. You know, like a typical child of the '80s and early '90s. We had four channels: ABC, CBS, NBC, and PBS.

If my mom thought I was watching too many mainstream cartoons, she would turn the channel to public broadcasting. More highbrow. Educational. Sometimes we would watch Sesame Street. I particularly liked Cookie Monster. I'm a cookie kind of guy.

After Sesame Street went off, a nasty blend of nightmare fuel entered. To me at least. A tall purple dinosaur singing about him loving me and me loving him (which I did not) came on the screen. Barney.

My shoulders shook with that memory as I first laid eyes on Sabrina. Natasha wasn't kidding. Sabrina was taller than me, broader than me, bigger than me. And I'm not a small person by any measure. She looked like she belonged in the WNBA. No, scratch that. She looked like she could be a lineman on any NFL football team.

She wore a light purple dress with green accents. That set off my Barney fear instinct. A matching set of pearl earrings and necklace contrasted with short, brown, tightly curled hair and dark skin. Her outfit looked well put together, to be honest.

Intelligent green eyes examined the break room before settling on the coffee display that wasn't there before.

"Hey," she snapped at the two women in the corner. They looked up from their phones. Sabrina pointed. "Where did the coffee come from?"

One woman pointed at me. "Him, I think."

They were sitting there when I came in, but they were so engrossed in their phones that they missed why I was here and either didn't hear or ignored my conversation with the executives.

"Oh," she said, turning to me. "Who are you?"

"I'm Clark."

"Oh, nice. Did you bring us coffee?"

"I did. I spoke with two of your employees yesterday at my store. One of them commented on the quality of coffee down here. So, I wanted to do my neighborly part and add a little cheer to your day."

She placed a hand over her heart. Her snarl turned into a smile. "Oh, well, thank you so much. It's been a tragic couple of days. This'll help with morale." She walked to the table with the coffee urns, rested a finger on her chin, tapped her foot, and grabbed a cup off the stack. As she poured herself a cup, she asked, "Who was it you saw yesterday?"

I didn't want to mention and give her any clue that I might know anything about what Natasha suspected of Sabrina and Chris skimming the tax money, so I said, "I don't recall. We were slammed busy yesterday despite the police investigation in the back and had so many people coming and going that I don't remember."

"Oh, okay," she said. I didn't catch a hint of suspicion in her tone. "What kind of coffee is this?"

I placed a hand on one urn and then the other. "This is a Columbian blend from Charleston Coffee Roasters, and this is the house blend from the Roasted Bean."

"Oh, the Roasted Bean in that brewery at Market Common?"

"That's the one."

"Let me try it," she said, pointing at the Roasted Bean carafe. "I think I've been there before."

I wasn't here to serve coffee, but judging by her authoritarian manner, she probably gets what she wants most of the time. That, and my Barney nervousness was kicking in. Besides, it gave me an excuse to start a conversation.

"Sure thing," I said and poured her a cup. I pointed to the accouterments. She shook two packets of Splenda (yuck) into the paper cup and gave it a stir.

"It's a tragedy about Paige." We stood with her between me and a window. She eclipsed the sunlight trying to get through.

She sipped and bobbed her head. "It is. It is. Very unexpected."

I wasn't sure how to tiptoe into a conversation about her and her snakelike partner possibly stealing from the resort, so I said, "I heard that Paige had an argument with someone in her office the night before her murder, but they weren't sure who with."

Her eyes locked on mine.

"Who told you that?" she said loud enough to cause the

women in the corner to look up from their phones.

I scratched my head. "I forget. It was one of you. I've talked to so many since yesterday. It's all a rush."

Her eyes weighed me, trying to determine if I was sincere or if she wanted to break me in half. Thankfully, she went the route of no bloodshed. "Yeah, there are a lot of rumors about Paige. I'd heard that one too. I wasn't here that night, so I wouldn't know."

"I'd met her before but hadn't gotten to know her."

"She was a sweet lady. The glue that held this place together. She was the go-between for our hourly workers working in the resort and the salaried staff working upstairs."

"Did you know her well?"

She looked away and tried to compose herself. "I did. I'd call us good friends. We hung out, went to shows and dinners, and vacationed a few times together."

"I'd heard that she was leaving for a trip the day she was killed."

"Mm-hmm. She was excited about it, too. Her son is a big Star Wars fan. They were going to surprise him with a trip to the new Galaxy's Edge attraction at Hollywood Studios in Orlando."

"Oh, man. I'm wanting to go to that."

"I don't know anything about it, personally. Never seen any of the movies."

I still get surprised when someone says they have never watched any Star Wars movies, even in passing. I almost had a kid once. "How old is her son?"

"He's four. She and her husband were going to put him in the car and not tell him where they were going until they got to

Orlando."

"Aww, that would have been awesome for him."

"Paige was a great parent." Sabrina wiped a tear from her eye with the back of her hand.

Between my brief interactions with Paige, knowing about her environmental activism, and now learning about her family, it struck me that her loss left a big hole in many lives.

"It's a shame," I said. "I don't know why anyone would want to kill her."

Her eyes darted to a vacant spot on the floor as she took a sip of coffee. "Me neither."

She had come into the break room for a reason, and it wasn't to talk to me. I figured that she was likely here to get a quick drink of something or grab some lunch and this conversation wouldn't run much longer. I needed to get to the point.

"What do you do here?" I asked.

"Work in the cash office. I handle the daily funds in and out."

"Ah, one of the least favorite parts of my job owning a bookstore."

Her lips parted in a smile, revealing a set of pearly whites and dimples on her cheeks. That made her seem less scary, but only by a little. "It's not bad. The pay is nice."

"Was it a big hassle to change your system to handle the change in hospitality taxes?"

The change in her expression was momentary, but enough. Like she went from casual conversation to a dark place. I knew I hit on something. "It was challenging."

"How so? I don't have to add hospitality taxes in my point-of-sale system, but I know that when there are changes to the tax rates, it's as easy as going in and adjusting the percentages."

"Well, it's not that easy here. Our POS system is downright archaic, like a middle schooler designed it after taking his first coding class. Thankfully, I'm not the one who implements those changes. That's upstairs. I count the receipts and make sure they jibe with what the system says we did in a day."

"Gotcha. So why was it challenging?"

"Oh, they had problems getting it right. It worked right if it was someone who hadn't visited here before, but if they had, and we pulled up their profile, they were charged with the old tax rate."

"What did you do when that happened?"

"It was a hassle. I'd have to calculate the difference in what they paid and what they owed and issue a refund and an apology."

"Oh, so something people working the desk might not know about?"

Her head bobbed. "Mm-hmm. Some of them would catch on and change it on the spot, others didn't. We were supposed to have a meeting yesterday to tell the staff about the mix-up, but you know."

The rug by my backdoor flashed before my eyes. "I do."

She glanced over my shoulder. "Look, it was nice meeting you and thanks for the coffee."

Chris strutted through the door. Serious as a heart attack. A man on a mission.

"Sabrina," he announced. She jolted and turned. "Meeting. Upstairs. Now."

"Why me? I have nothing to do with what you all do up there."

"You do now."

"What do you mean?"

He glared at the two low-level workers in the corner, intent on their phones now more than ever. I couldn't blame them. The janitor returned with a broom and swept near the door.

"You're getting…" He broke off what he was saying and looked at me. "Hey, I recognize you. You're the guy from the downtown development meeting last night."

"Guilty," I said.

"You're the one who found Paige."

"I am."

The sleeves on his dress shirt were rolled back with that executive-who-means-business look revealing matching barbed-wire tattoos around his wrists. The sweat on his furrowed brow and heaving barrel chest made me think he had just done a quick fifty pushups out in the hall before walking in. The man was a walking hulk of testosterone.

Which is why his next action shocked me.

"Come here," he said and wrapped me in a bear hug.

That was unexpected.

CHAPTER
TWELVE

For a man of average height, Chris possessed enormous hands. Their grip on my back suggested calloused fingers and meaty palms, as though countless hours of manual labor existed in their past. They kneaded the muscles in my back while he gripped me. I pictured him as a blacksmith. He smelled of expensive cologne and sweat.

"Man, must have been scary," he said, breaking the embrace.

"It was definitely unexpected."

"I'm sure. Look, Sabrina and I need to get upstairs for a meeting, but I'd love to chat with you later. Our VP, Martin, had me go to that meeting in his place. I liked what you and that other girl had to say. You had some nice ideas."

"Marilyn."

"Okay, I didn't catch her name last night," he said and then repeated, "Marilyn."

"She's the perfect example of not judging a book by its cover. Sharp as a tack." Speaking of books and covers, I reevaluated my initial assessment of Chris. Natasha's description of him and his appearance painted different pictures from my first literal contact.

"Of all the people there," he said, "you two were the only ones who didn't have greedy objectives."

I shrugged. "I hope that doing things for the greater good will help my bottom line here, anyway. Why not work together to build a better Myrtle Beach?"

"You sound like a politician. Ever considered running for office?"

"No, no, no. I'm content where I am."

He took a step back and smiled. It was frightening, but it was a smile. "I admire that. It's not every day you meet someone like you in our circles."

"Wait," Sabrina said. "He's the poor guy from yesterday? I figured you were just a nice guy bringing us some coffee."

"Why can't I be both?" I said.

"If I were you after what happened yesterday," Sabrina said, "I'd go buy a case of wine to get those mental images out of my head. Go see a therapist, something. Not come down here, and sure as heck not come to work."

"Keeping busy takes my mind off of it." Except for when I'm trying to figure out who killed her.

"Listen," Chris said, jabbing a finger at my shoulder. "I'm serious. Let's talk later." He reached into his back pocket. "Here's my card. Take it. Call me. There's a bottle of Belle Meade bourbon up in my office we can share a drink with."

I was getting a collection of business cards from the last two days. "Thanks. I'll do that. I'm a bourbon kind of guy, anyway."

He clasped me on the shoulder. "You and I will get along fine. Come on, Sabrina, they await."

She stepped away from the table. The eclipse ended. Sunlight streamed back into the room.

"It was nice meeting you," she said to me as she thundered past.

"Same here," I said.

Chris escorted her through the door with a paw on the small of her back. Not that there was anything small about her. Natasha said Chris had been in prison. For what, I did not know. Maybe he's reformed or something. Seemed like a genuinely nice guy.

The two women must have finished watching everything on YouTube. They got up and followed Chris and Sabrina from the break room. Only the janitor and I remained.

I took one last look at the coffee set up. I'd come back later to get my urns.

As I passed by the janitor, I said, "Hey, I put two jugs of fresh coffee on that table over there. Help yourself."

He stopped sweeping and tipped his cap to me. The name "James" was screen printed on the breast pocket of his charcoal gray twill uniform. Gray hair curled out of the edges of his hat. A slight hunch in his back led me to believe that he's spent a lifetime pushing that broom. His salt and pepper mustache twitched. "Thank you, sir. I appreciate it. I'll sneak in a cup as soon as I get finished with my task here," he said, tipping the broom.

"Sounds good," I said. "Mind if I ask you a few questions since there's nobody in here?"

He scanned the room before ducking his head out into the hall, looking both ways. Probably didn't want to get caught not working. "Sure, sure."

I don't have any official standing with the police. If someone whom I wanted to question didn't want to talk to me, it would require finesse on my part to get them to open up. That this man and Natasha would speak to me showed me how much these people loved Paige.

"I'll be quick. Are you normally here this time of day?"

"Yessir. I'm here in the mornings, except for Mondays and Tuesdays. That's my weekend."

"Gotta get it where you can. I try to take Sundays and Mondays off."

"I wish I could get a Sunday every once in a while, but the staffing agency says I have to be here on their busiest days."

"Oh, so you're not employed by OceanScapes?"

"No, sir. They contract that out."

"Why do they do that?"

"Beats me. My guess is so they can pass out fewer bonus checks at the end of the year."

Whatever the reason, it seemed like an odd arrangement. "So, you weren't here yesterday for all the hubbub surrounding Paige?"

"Not during the morning. They called all of them in but forgot about me and my crew until later."

"Yeah, two of their employees came into my bookstore while they were waiting."

"Bookstore?"

"Yeah, I own the Myrtle Beach Reads up the street."

"No way." He pointed at my chest. "Are you the poor dude who found Paige?"

"I am." I wondered how long I would have that question asked of me.

"Saw that on the news. That must have been a shock."

"Something I will never forget. Look, I was watching you

out of the corner of my eye while I was talking to Chris and Sabrina. You seemed like you were invisible to everyone."

He smiled, revealing a gold tooth. "That's how it is. I'm the invisible man. The fly on the wall."

"I bet you hear a lot of things."

He leaned in close. "You wouldn't believe some of the stories I could tell you."

"What do you know about Paige?"

"Why do you want to know?"

"Just common human interest."

He hesitated, shifted on the balls of his feet, and seemed to judge me. "I'll tell you what I heard."

"What's that?"

"Paige and some owners were on the outs."

"How so?"

"There're rumors floating around that she's not happy with the people wanting to buy this place and is doing her best to talk them out of it."

"Does she have a stake in ownership?"

"Not that I know of. She carried a lot of clout. Been here since Day One."

"She seemed like an influencer," I said. I am not trained in interrogation techniques, but I've read hundreds of mystery books and wrote adventure novels where I had to piece together clues to solve a puzzle. The pieces revolving around Paige were forming a picture. Getting them to fit together would be the hard part.

If the tension between her and an owner had escalated to where someone wanted Paige dead, then they would possess the access they needed to get into her office. They also would have known about the cameras in the stairwell. Hmm.

I asked, "Do you have access to the upstairs offices?"

"I do. I clean them and empty the trash in the mornings before they get here."

"Does someone do the cleaning for you when you're off?"

"Of course. Wouldn't be prudent to allow the bigwigs to wallow in a sty all day, would it?"

The thought of Chris sitting around in a mud pit during James' days off made me laugh. "True, true. So, there was someone here yesterday morning in place of you?"

"Julieta was. Poor girl. She gets in and heads upstairs and finds a mess in Paige's office."

"What time did she get here?"

He shrugged. "I'm not sure. You'd have to ask her. We're supposed to be here about 8:30."

When I called the police after finding Paige's body, the clock on my phone read a few minutes before eight. I stopped wearing a watch years ago, except for the rare occasions when I wore a suit. I thought of it as being on 'island time.' That brought to mind a question for me to ask Detective Gomez. "Is Julieta working now?"

"Oh no. She was so shaken up that they told her to go home after she saw that office and talked to the police."

"Do you know what she saw?"

"She isn't supposed to talk to anyone about it."

"But…"

He leaned in and whispered, "I heard that the room was wrecked. Paper thrown everywhere. Chairs tossed aside. A smear of blood on the carpet behind the desk. A mess."

Not knowing the setup of her office, I had my first visual of the crime. The scene of Paige's demise tried to play in my head, but it was blurry. Like an old video camera recording from the eighties. There were a couple of ways to sharpen those images.

"Did you or one of your coworkers clean it up?"

"They haven't asked us to, and I'm not about to volunteer to do it."

"Didn't they open up the offices? How would they do that?"

"I was up there a few minutes ago after they granted permission to return. Yellow police tape was strung up on her door."

"All the offices are open except for hers?"

"It appeared so."

I tapped my foot. "Can you get in touch with Julieta?"

"I don't work with her that often. Don't really know her."

A potential roadblock. Perhaps there was another way to contact her.

Three people entered the break room. James and I separated to let them pass. I took that as my cue to leave.

"Thank you for your time, sir."

He tipped his cap. "No problem, sir. Have a great day."

"You too."

The new knot of workers was at the table against the wall getting coffee. I made sure everything was in order and left.

As I went through the hall, headed back toward the front desk, I checked my phone to see a text from my parents.

They needed help.

CHAPTER
THIRTEEN

Natasha hurried from behind the counter and grabbed me on my way out.

"Hey," she said. "Sorry I had to leave you alone in the break room. Had to get back to the desk."

I held up a placating hand. "No need to apologize. I understand. I didn't expect you to hang around while I did that. Nor would I have wanted you to. From what you said, there would have been zero chance Chris or Sabrina would have talked to me if you were present."

"That's a relief," she said. "Were you able to talk to either of them?"

"I spoke to both."

"Did you learn anything?"

"Let me ask you a question first. Who handles your point of sale system?"

"What is that?"

I tried to think about how to explain that to a person where English was her second language. While she spoke good English, there were things she didn't quite seem to understand. "You know when you go to accept a payment from a guest? Where you noticed the discrepancy in the hospitality tax?" She nodded. "That's the point of sale."

"Oh, I get it."

"Do you know who controls that system?"

"I'm not sure."

"Okay. Sabrina said that the taxes would be wrong on returning guests. Their profiles wouldn't be updated with the new tax percentages."

"Yeah, so?"

I knew what I was about to say would disappoint her. "Sabrina said she would issue a refund and an apology when that happened, and that some clerks would catch and correct the mistake."

Her shoulders sagged as she looked out a window over my shoulder. "What about the taxes that are now supposed to go to the city?"

"She didn't mention that."

Natasha tapped a foot and chewed on a fingernail. "What did you think of them?"

"Honestly, they seemed like pleasant people. Despite appearances."

"I'm telling you," she grabbed my arm and squeezed, "they can't be trusted."

People often put their best foot forward when first meeting others. Because you only get one chance, you know. But what if that best foot isn't a true foot? You can't always trust the first impression.

"Sabrina said that she and Paige were good friends," I said. "They did stuff together all the time."

"Can't friends have arguments?"

"Sabrina seemed hesitant when I mentioned anyone having

a reason to kill Paige."

"See, there's reason enough to keep digging."

Why me? I wanted to ask. "How long have they been with OceanScapes? Sabrina and Chris?"

Natasha's brow crinkled. "Hmm. Sabrina's been here for a while. A long time. Chris came on after I began working here. A year or two, I guess."

"Intriguing. Chris asked me to come back to his office later for a drink. I have to come back anyway to retrieve my coffee urns."

"You're leaving?"

"Yeah, I need to go help my mom with something. She said it's urgent."

"Do they live nearby?"

"Not far. Down in Surfside. A fifteen-minute drive from here if the stoplights cooperate."

She patted my arm. "Family comes first. I will speak to you later."

I hurried back to the store and made sure Karen came in for her shift. Hers and Margaret's shifts overlapped until mid-afternoon, meaning that I had a few free hours. They said they had a handle on things—which I knew they did—and I drove down Kings Highway a few minutes later.

I called Gomez along the way. She said I had to be quick.

"You said you had a lead," I said. "Mind if I ask what that is?"

"Paige had been getting death threats."

"Who from?"

"We're not sure yet. We got into her personal and work emails and found them. At first, they came at random times, months apart. Then they started coming in increasing frequency in recent months. They come from a unique email address every time. The names are always obscured. Gibberish. A bunch of random letters and numbers from equally random email providers. We are working on tracking them back now."

"How frequent?"

"In the past three months, it's been once a week."

"What's the content of the threats?"

"They are all the same. 'We're going to kill you.'"

"Who do you think they are from?"

"I don't want to speculate, but we have some ideas."

"Makes sense. I've heard that oil people made threats to her in the past."

"No comment."

"Had she come forward to you all with these recent threats?"

"Not to us. She'd told her husband about them, though. They didn't take them seriously since they came after the offshore drilling talk calmed down."

I smiled. "There's your comment on your 'no comment.'"

She let out an exasperated sigh. "You got me. Have you learned anything?"

"I did. I heard she was arguing with someone in her office last night."

"Really? With whom?"

"This was told to me by Marilyn, who owns We Got Issues. She said one of the OceanScapes employees told her about the supposed confrontation, but he didn't see who it was."

"Who said this to her?"

"I think the kid's name is Solomon."

"Noted. I'll have to find him. Thanks for the tip." She breathed into the phone. "Look, Clark. I'm not going to tell you to stop what you're doing, but I'm also not going to condone it either. We're chasing slim leads in a case where there's not much evidence. Investigating a murder can be dangerous. You could also screw something up, tip off a suspect, and they get away with it. Be careful."

She ended the call without so much as a goodbye. If Moody was with her, I'm sure he listened and added an insightful grunt.

* * *

My parents sold their home up north a few years ago up and bought a big, brand new two-story place in Surfside Beach just south of Myrtle Beach. The snowy winters were hard on their bodies as they got older. The cold made their bones hurt. Particularly my mom's. She had two bouts with cancer ten years apart. Her radiation treatments on this latest round ended a couple of weeks ago and she was still undergoing the healing process.

Doctors found tumors on the back of her tongue and roof of her mouth. It was a cancer that typically afflicted smokers called squamous cell carcinoma. Except that she never smoked a cigarette in her life. It baffled us as much as her doctors.

The combination of radiation and chemotherapy treatments almost killed her the first time. The process ravaged her body, leaving her weakened and frail. She had a reputation as a fighter before cancer. She kicked cancer's butt. We thought it was gone.

It returned ten years later.

This time, doctors caught it early. After a minor surgery and six weeks of radiation treatments, she was on the mend. Chemotherapy wasn't needed this time.

They were getting up in years and my dad kept me busy doing things around their place. I didn't mind. The task took my mind off other things.

Many of their neighbors were retirees who needed odds and ends taken care of that they couldn't do themselves or didn't know how. They caught word that I helped my parents do this and that and, before I knew it, I was getting calls from them to help around their houses. Thanks, Mom and Dad.

Mom greeted me at the door with a hug and showed me in.

If it weren't for Mom, I doubt that I would be where I am today. From an early age, I recalled her being an avid reader. It seemed like she was always reading books by Agatha Christie and Nora Roberts when she wasn't watching Murder She Wrote, Perry Mason, and more recently, Monk.

I read nothing outside of the classroom as a kid. I mostly played outdoors. Basketball, baseball, football, hiking in the woods, etc. until one spring when I was thirteen, I caught the flu and was laid up in bed over one weekend.

That Sunday, one network played the first three—and the only three at that time—Star Wars movies. I had heard of them but never watched any. I watched the first one, and by the time Luke Skywalker blew up the Death Star, I was mesmerized. I watched the other two and loved them. I wanted more. This was before the Internet and digital streaming, so I figured I'd have to check the TV Guide to see when it came on again. Remember that magazine?

Mom did the grocery shopping every Friday. I came home

from school at the end of the next week and found a book on the counter. Normally, I would have ignored it. But this wasn't any other book. It was a Star Wars book by Timothy Zahn called The Last Command. It was the last novel in a trilogy, but I did not care. I consumed the book that weekend and wanted to read the two which came before it.

Before I knew it, I had a stack of science fiction novels by my bed. When I couldn't find a book, I went to the library.

Over the next few years, I grew an extensive collection. Little did I know that would be the first investment in a bookstore that wouldn't open for another twenty years.

They gave me stock for the shelves and knowledge. All because of Mom picking up one book from Kroger's.

"Sorry to bother you," she apologized. Her blonde hair was cut in a bob that hung above the shoulders. Her clothes appeared two sizes too big because of weight loss during her radiation treatments. She hadn't been able to eat solid food in weeks.

"It's okay." I gave her a hug. She melted into my embrace. I lived three minutes away in a different neighborhood, so I was over here often. "What's up? You said it was urgent."

"It's for your dad."

"What's wrong?" Dad's health had been declining in recent years after suffering a slight stroke, which limited some use of the right side of his body. He couldn't write anymore. Mom had to sign all his checks and documents. He had a noticeable limp that his doctor said he should use a cane for. The cane sat in the corner of their garage behind old moving boxes.

"He needs you to figure out how to record the game for him tonight."

They used to live in an extreme point of southern Ohio in Proctorville, across the river from Huntington, West Virginia. It was a pleasant enough town to grow up in, but remaining in the area after high school was not the plan for me. We vacationed in Myrtle Beach most years, and I dreamed of moving here as a teen. I applied to one college in high school: Coastal Carolina in nearby Conway. They accepted me. I went for four years and earned my degree and only went back to Ohio to visit family and friends. With my parents down here now, I didn't foresee any return trips in my future.

We lived close to the Marshall University campus across the river in Huntington, and Dad was a huge Thundering Herd fan. I didn't care for them. Never did. I was more of an Ohio State guy.

The Marshall basketball team rarely played on a television station around here. When they did, it was almost always at odd times. Usually a late game. Past Dad's bedtime, which varied depending on when the sun went down.

He was used to watching television via an antenna and picking up local stations. This new digital era passed him by. I was their go-to for technical support.

I followed Mom past a luxurious kitchen — granite counters, stainless steel appliances, gas range, expensive coffeemaker — to the living room. Dad had his feet up on a white leather loveseat, watching the huge, curved television on a white TV stand. He gripped a stone coffee cup with the word "Papaw" engraved on it.

"Hey, pipsqueak," he said as I entered the room, although I outgrew him in middle school. He still possessed a beer belly from his younger days and had a clean-shaven head.

"Hey, Dad. Mom says you need some help."

He tilted his head toward the TV. "I need the game recorded tonight."

I helped get their cable package setup when they moved in and showed them several times how to record programs. I don't know if they didn't understand the process or wanted to give me something to do. Surely this could have waited until later.

"No problem," I said. "Let me see your remote."

As he reached it to me, Mom asked if I would like some coffee. I said I would and a few minutes later, after setting the game to record, I sat on the opposite couch from them sipping coffee brewed from a pod. Not my favorite brewing method, but it works for many.

The television displayed a replay of a college basketball game from yesterday between two teams that held little interest to Dad. He watched every basketball game he could. He loved amateur basketball and did not care for the NBA. I was the opposite.

Mom took a sip from her Murrell's Inlet mug and said to me as I was in mid sip, "Why did I have to find out from the local news that you found a dead person?"

I almost choked on the coffee. Oops.

"I'm sorry," I said. "My mistake. I was so busy yesterday and so tired last night after I went home, I had a quick bite to eat and went straight to bed."

"That's okay," she said. "I'm sure you would have told us about it."

"Yeah," Dad said without taking his eyes off the screen, "after that poor girl got put in the ground."

Mom slapped him in the arm. "Now Lloyd. Don't talk that

way."

"Yes, dear," he said and went back to his game.

"Now tell me all about it, Clark," she said.

I related what happened, leaving out no details, and told her about my little investigation. She'd read and seen almost every type of murder imaginable. Jessica Fletcher and Adrian Monk would have met their equal if they had to match crime-solving wits with mom. At least, I imagined so.

She looked thoughtful as she took a long sip of coffee. After smacking her lips and clearing her throat, she said, "There are three big questions you need to answer. More questions will branch off of those."

"What are they?" I asked.

She raised a first, second, and third finger. "Means, motive, and opportunity. Who had the means to kill her? Who wanted her dead? Who could have been there yesterday morning?"

"The first one is easy," I said. "Somebody hit her with something hard."

"No, not so easy. What did they hit her with? Did the concavity of her head suggest the type or shape of the object that killed her?"

"I don't know," I admitted. "I tried not to look too close at the deformation."

"What did the medical examiner say?"

"I don't know."

"Find out," she said. "Then you will know what to look for."

"My guess is that the killer disposed of the murder weapon."

"Don't make guesses. Only deal with facts. Guesses could have you looking in the wrong direction when the real thing passes you by."

"Gotcha." I whipped out my phone to take notes.

"Let's forget the murder weapon for a moment. Let's say you're the killer and she's dead, lying on the floor. What do you do?"

I closed my eyes and tried to see what I imagined Paige's office would look like. I needed to get a glimpse when I shared a whiskey with Chris later.

"If I'm the murderer, I think about how I'm going to get out of there without someone noticing. I look down, see the rug, and have the bright idea to roll her up in it. There's probably one person at the front desk, but it is in a separate part of the building."

"Find out who was there."

Natasha might know. I made a note. "I will."

She drummed her fingers on the sofa armrest like a patient professor. "Good. Go on."

"She was a small woman. I carry her down the stairs over my shoulder like I would with a rug and leave the building."

"Then what? How did he get her the three blocks up to your bookstore? Did he carry her? Put her in the trunk of a car and drop her off?"

"No to the last one. If I'm going to put her in a trunk, I'm going to take her far away from OceanScapes."

"Then the killer was exposed."

"That was my thought. So, either he carried her or had her in the back of a truck. The owner of the t-shirt shop a couple doors down was in and out of her rear alcove throwing away boxes. He must have seen her, got spooked, and ditched her at my door."

"Then what?"

"I guess he returned to OceanScapes and went back to work."

She wagged a finger. "What did I tell you about guessing?"

"Don't do it. Right."

"You have a few questions branching off 'means'. What killed her? How did the killer transport the body? Where was the killer taking her? Was your store his goal? Where did the killer go after that?"

I punched those questions into a note app on my phone.

"If the killer carried her," Mom said, "who is strong enough to do that?"

One person popped into my head. "I haven't seen or met everyone who works there yet, but I've seen a couple strong dudes."

"Look into them. Let's move onto motive. Who wanted her dead?"

"I know of three motives. The police detective told me that Paige has been receiving death threats from oil companies."

"Why would they want her dead?"

"She helped squash their plans to drill offshore."

"Money."

"Lots of it, apparently. Moving on, I was told that there had been friction between Paige and the ownership group over a possible sale of the resort."

"Oh?"

"I haven't spoken to anyone with intimate knowledge of what is happening, but the word is that she was pushing against it because of something to do with the people wanting to buy it."

"Do you think her pushback was reason enough to kill her?"

I shrugged. "Dunno. Don't have enough details."

"Find out if one of the actual owners or prospective buyers had enough reason to do it. What else?"

"Natasha told Paige about a coworker who she thought was stealing from the company the night before she was killed. I heard someone else say they heard Paige get into a shouting match after the alleged embezzler left for the night."

"Any idea who with?"

"Not at present, but I know the person I need to speak to who heard that shouting match."

"Let's get this straight. You have the embezzler, the oil company assassin, and someone involved in the potential sale of the resort?"

"That's the way I figure it."

She drained the last of her coffee and set the empty mug on a side table. Dad's chin lolled forward to his chest as he snored softly.

"Must be an exciting game," she said and steepled her fingers. "Now, opportunity. Who could have been able to do this?"

"That I'm not sure about," I admitted. "The employees have keycards to gain access to different areas of the building. There should be a system in place for them to track every move."

"Were there many employees there at the time of her death?"

"Natasha said that there couldn't have been many."

"Then it shouldn't be difficult to see where they were and if any of them came near her office."

That thought hadn't occurred to me. I held up a hand. "I

know. I'll check."

Mom's healing process was going well. Her skin pallor was almost back to normal. The pain had subsided by a few degrees, but she still showed nasty effects. Such as a wracking cough. Like now.

She hacked into a gingham handkerchief, waking Dad. He jolted and patted her back during the attack. This was the painful part. These attacks could last for several minutes and leave her exhausted. There was little I could do to help.

Dad gave me a stern nod. I knew the signal.

I departed a minute later with more questions than answers, but now I had a few ideas about what I should do next. Thanks to Mom.

CHAPTER
FOURTEEN

Life is full of decisions. Big ones. Little ones. Ones that change your life. Ones that impact your day. Do I get out of bed today? What's for breakfast? Do I need to take a shower? Should I call my mom today or keep putting it off? Should I put more money into my 401K? What color shirt should I wear? Do I watch the news or old Bugs Bunny cartoons?

The choices are endless. "Overchoice" is the term sometimes used. I prefer "option paralysis." The mind can't decide when confronted with a multitude of options. Whatever it is, I have it.

I stared at the array of options in front of me while trying to decide if any of these could change my life. The smallest choice can cause the biggest ripples. The butterfly effect.

I've been sitting here, staring at the McDonald's drive-thru menu for a solid five minutes trying to reach a decision. The line of cars grew. They had to wait. I was here first.

The woman in the BMW behind me honked her horn for the third time and gave me the middle finger for the second time. It doesn't help when someone breaks my concentration like that; you know?

"Sir, come on," the muffled voice said through the speaker below the menu board. "Are you ready to order, yet?"

I stared at the choices one last time. "Okay, give me a bacon, egg, and cheese biscuit, hash browns, and a large sweet tea."

She read off my total and followed it with something that sounded like "Thank you, Jesus," but I'm not sure.

That was my go-to order at this McDonald's near the airport. They always got this one right. Whoever made their biscuits during the mid-day hours was masterful, as I knew from experience.

I pulled forward and saw relief on the faces of the drivers behind me, except for the woman next in line. She glared and held her hand out the window with the middle finger upraised.

I checked my mirror as I got to the payment window. The woman in the BMW had withdrawn her hand, ostensibly so she could gather her payment, but still shot me evil looks as she gathered her form of payment.

"That'll be $5.82 please," the exasperated employee at the window said.

I handed her a debit card. "Hey, I'm going to pay this woman's ticket in the car behind me, too."

The employee craned her neck out the window. "Okay, sir."

"Give me both receipts, please."

"Sure." She swiped the card and then handed me two long receipts with surveys for a free chicken biscuit without saying "thank you."

I moved the Jeep forward, looking back as the employee told the woman I had paid for her meal. She leaned out the window, smiled and waved, this time with all five fingers. Her cheeks were red.

When I arrived at the second window, the server held a white bag with golden arches and a large cup out for me to grab.

The only direction you can turn is right, coming out of this McDonald's. I made a few zigzags as I returned to the store in case the lady had a Glock in her glove compartment.

As the ocean and resorts flowed past to my right, my solitary lunch reminded me about how losing Autumn left a hole in my heart and life. I missed her every minute of every day. I reminded myself every morning that it was okay for me to be happy. She would want it that way. Her pillow remains in the same place. She loved her pillow almost as much as me. The scent of her perfume lingered on it for months after she was gone. Even long after her essence faded, I still rolled over on lonely, sleepless nights hoping to put my arm around her waist. She was a small woman and could snuggle herself into my arms like a little nesting doll.

Myrtle Beach was known for its multitude of restaurants, and we explored as many of them as we could. They were reminders of our life together. We had our favorites, but I couldn't return to them. She hated McDonald's, so I knew that was one place I could go without sparking any melancholic memories. My waistline resented me for it.

We had a tradition of having dinner at Villa Romana every year on our wedding anniversary. I tried going there on what would have been our anniversary to carry on the tradition but walked out as soon as I entered. I couldn't do it. It was too difficult. I cried into a Whopper on the way home that night.

There were no customers in the store when I arrived. I checked in with Karen and as soon as I walked into to my office, Marilyn called.

"Hey," she said. "He's here."

"Solomon?"

"Yeah."

"Great. Try to keep him there. I'll be up in a minute."

I practically ran out of the store and started up Ocean Boulevard. The sun was high in a cloudless sky. Coolness settled across my bare forearms. Although midweek during the offseason was light in tourists, there was a surprising number of people milling about. Several stood out as out-of-towners, but many might be locals who don't venture near downtown Myrtle Beach during the warm months.

Tables with chairs, lamp posts, and flags billowing in the salty breeze lined the wide Boardwalk. An expansive area with several beach volleyball courts a stone's throw from the ocean sat empty. The crave-able aroma of funnel cakes intermingled with hot dogs, salt, and cigarette smoke permeated the air.

Most people wore smiles. Those who didn't were harried parents chasing after toddlers. That was almost me.

One aspect of life that I loved about the Myrtle Beach Boardwalk and Downtown MB is that you see many of the same faces over and over. Workers, business owners, maintenance workers, city employees, police officers, fire fighters. All of them. It breeds familiarity. When life gets hectic during the summer months, you can always find a friendly face who understands what you're going through.

I frequent many of the restaurants during the busy season as I don't have time go home and cook meals for myself. I rarely leave the store until well past closing. I'll lock the door and realize that it's been ten hours or more since I last ate. That would lead to me taking a quick jaunt up the Boardwalk and grab a bite and a beer.

On the way to Marilyn's shop I saw several familiar faces. A girl who works at the Nathan's Hot Dog stand rushed by on her way to work. Several of the city groundskeepers were grooming the foliage along the Boardwalk, dropping clippings into a bin towed by a city golf cart. One fella had a wife who was a regular at the store.

Just another day on the Boardwalk.

In between the large open area between 8th and 9th Avenues, a guy walked fifty yards ahead of me on the sidewalk closest to the ocean. He wore a gray custodial outfit. I crossed the street and fell in step behind him. Vacant beach volleyball courts passed by to my left. Waves crashed on the shore.

The man in front of me veered right past the volleyball courts and entered a wood panel faced dive bar. It was a place I had never been in before. The clientele had a reputation of being a collection of shady characters. The food was supposed to be good, though.

I glimpsed enough of his face as he opened the door to recognize him. He was the janitor from OceanScapes. I racked my brain trying to come up with his name. James, I think. Natasha told me he was everywhere. I guess that meant on the Boardwalk as well.

I strolled past the Ripley's Believe It or Not museum and opened the door to We Got Issues a few spots away. Blowup cardboard cutouts of the most popular superheroes and villains crowded the front window display. Marilyn liked to mix comic book universes. Batman and the Joker hung out with the Avengers in one window. The other window had Superman, Wolverine, Green Lantern, Spiderman, and Captain America arranged around a poker table. She changed the arrangement often. I never knew what to expect. Having a scowling Batman next to Iron Man earned a chuckle from me.

Racks containing thousands of issues of comic books sat on tables around the perimeter and in the middle of the store. Several more superhero and pop fiction cardboard cutouts were stuck to black walls in interesting configurations. My favorite was of a young Luke Skywalker who seemed to gaze wistfully at Betty Boop sitting on a table in a provocative pose.

Marilyn still had her hair tied off into pigtails, but she added a pair of glasses that looked straight from a vintage store for her look today. Her t-shirt was of the Golden Girls posing and dressed like the Teenage Mutant Ninja Turtles. She stood behind a cash register to the left of the door as I entered.

She smiled and pointed to the back corner of the store. "Hey, Clark. He's back there."

A rail-thin black kid with hunched shoulders, his back to us, leafed through a box of clear poly plastic bagged comics.

"Thanks, Marilyn."

I walked to his corner and started digging through a box of Green Lantern comics. He glanced over at me and went back to his search.

"Hey man," I said. "Does she have the latest Incredible Hulk in there?"

Big brown eyes swung up at me. "You like the Hulk?"

"Mm-hmm."

"Get out. Me too. He's my favorite."

"Cool. Who's your favorite Hulk actor?"

He thought for a moment, tapping the side of the box containing The Incredible Hulk issues. "I like the guy from the Avengers movies. Mark something-or-other."

"Ruffalo?"

"Yeah, that's him. Who do you like?'

"Me? I go way back. Lou Ferrigno."

The gravity of his face moved to the center. Wrinkles appeared on his forehead and chin. "Who is that?"

"He was the original Hulk, way before special effects. He was a body builder with muscles on top of muscles who they painted green and put some purple lipstick on him."

"The real deal, huh?"

"Yup. Didn't need CGI for him. You should look him up."

"I'll do that." He whipped out his phone and I helped him spell the name as he typed in a search. "Whoa. He's huge!"

"You'll have to find that old show online."

"Thanks, mister. I'm sure I can find it somewhere."

He had short hair and a cleft nose. His clothes looked two sizes too big. Like his mama bought them that way expecting for him to grow. Except that he was almost past puberty.

"I notice you work down at OceanScapes," I said.

He reached up and felt the resort logo on his chest. "Yeah, I do."

"Sorry about Paige."

He turned back to the comics, not wanting to make eye contact. His shoulders sagged even more. "Yeah, thanks, man. She was like a second mom. Maybe an aunt. She did so much for me."

"Like what?"

"She gave me a chance. Mom is disabled. Dad can't keep a job. My brothers and sisters aren't old enough to work."

"That's tough."

"Yup. I applied there and a buncha other places as soon as I turned fourteen. Paige called me in. Heard my story. Hired me on the spot."

"That's nice. She must have seen something in you beyond your background that told her you would be a good hire."

His chest puffed up. I earned his respect with that last statement.

"You from around here?"

"Yeah, I own the bookstore down the street."

"Cool, cool. Wait." He turned to look at me. His eyes were bloodshot. "Are you the dude who found her?"

"I am."

"Whoa. That must have been insane. Finding her and all."

"It was crazy."

We were quiet as we stood side-by-side, flipping through comics.

After a minute, he sniffled and said, "I wanted to talk to her the night before she was killed but didn't get the chance."

"Why is that?"

"I was waiting to clock out there outside of her office and wanted to ask her about getting off one weekend in November, when I heard her arguing with someone."

"What time was this?"

"Uh, around seven. Why?"

"I'm doing some checking is all."

"Like, you're investigating her murder? I thought that's what the cops did?"

"They do, but I'm curious how she ended up at my store."

"Wouldn't they figure that out themselves?"

Smart kid. Good question. It brought me up short. "Yeah, I guess they would. Maybe. I'm not the type of person who waits around for answers. I like to figure out things myself."

He jabbed a thumb at his chest. "Me too!"

"I figured as much. You look like a man who takes matters into his own hands. Have you spoken to the police about this?"

"No, not yet. I was at school when they called everyone in to do that. No one told me I needed to."

"You probably slipped through the cracks."

He stuck a thumb into his chest. "Yeah, no one figures the kid would know anything."

"They'll get to you. There's a lot for them to sort out. You've gotta be on their list. So, what happened?"

"I got off at seven and went up to clock out early. When I got there, I heard Paige and another woman yelling at each other."

"Oh, really?"

"Yeah. I was like, crap, what do I do? I wondered if my question could wait. Paige was a nice person, but intense, you know? She was the sweetest person in the world, but when it was time to get serious, she could be intimidating. Those eyes, man. Those eyes."

"What about them? The eyes?"

"They were like this really bright green that could stare a hole in your soul if you didn't watch out. Like laser beams."

"Hmm. So, what did you do?"

"I clocked out. I knew I was supposed to work today anyway, so I'd ask her then. I knew that schedule wouldn't get made for a while."

It was a striking reminder to me to not procrastinate. You never know when opportunity will pass you by, or when you won't get a chance to speak to someone again. An image of Autumn floated through my head.

"Did you see who she was arguing with?"

"Yeah. Paige's door opened right as I hit the clock and that hot Natasha girl from the front desk came storming out."

CHAPTER
FIFTEEN

I raced back to the store, not knowing what to think. Another
name to add to the suspect list.

Natasha? She seemed so sweet. Innocent. Maybe a little
cold. Could be a reflection of her cultural background.

Come to think of it, when I revealed to her and Gloria that
Paige was dead, Gloria took it hard while Natasha remained
stoic. Like the news didn't surprise her. Now I didn't know if I
could trust her.

I called the OceanScapes front desk, hoping that Natasha
was still there.

"OceanScapes Resort," she answered on the third ring.

"Hey, I need to ask you something," I said, crossing over Joe
White Avenue. The ocean roiled to my left. A car honked its
horn to my right at some landlubbers who jaywalked in front of
them with their eyes intent on their phones. "I don't want to do
it while you're at work. When do you get off?"

"Who is this?" she asked.

"It's Clark."

"Oh, sorry. I wasn't expecting your call. Sorry. I get off in
about ten, fifteen minutes."

"Think you could swing by the store after you're done?"

* * *

I bounded up the three steps onto the front deck of the shopping strip with Myrtle Beach Reads. Ceiling fans swung in lazy arcs overhead on a honey-stained reclaimed wood ceiling. The heavy green cast iron tables outside of the Boardwalk Creamery sat empty.

I plopped down in a chair and watched the waves of the Atlantic roll onshore across the street. The smell of baking waffle cones caused my stomach to gurgle. It was about time for an afternoon snack and coffee. The McDonald's didn't stick with me for as long as I had hoped. That's the price I paid when making food decisions on the run. The foods I crave are often the ones I ate in my teens and early twenties. The ones responsible adults should stay away from. That's why I rarely picked where Autumn and I ate for the fifteen years of our marriage. It's something I still haven't gotten used to after losing her.

My shoulders ached. Mom's admonition as a kid to "stand up straight" never took. Now my chiropractor tells me that most of my back and neck issues would go away if I stopped slouching. With treatments over many, many years. Sigh. Maybe it was the weight of this case bringing soreness to my shoulders and neck.

What were Natasha and Paige arguing about? Could I trust Natasha to tell the truth?

I watched the waves crash for a few minutes while waiting. Their staccato rhythm did wonders for the soul.

My phone rang. It was Gomez.

"Hey," she said when I answered. "Sorry about rushing you

earlier. I was in the middle of something."

"No, it's okay. I learned who Paige was arguing with the night before her death."

"Ah. Excellent work, Clark."

"I talked to the Solomon kid, who said he was upstairs in the OceanScapes offices the night before Paige's death, around seven. He said he heard Paige arguing with someone in her office and saw a girl who works at the front desk storm out of there a moment later."

"Interesting. Did you get the name?"

"Yeah. Natasha."

"We spoke to her, but she didn't mention that. Did he say what the argument was about?"

"He didn't know."

"I'll find out."

I might be hindering a police investigation by not telling Gomez, but I didn't want to betray Natasha's trust. Yet.

"Another question," I said. "When did the cameras get spray painted? Before or after Paige arrived?"

"It was after. The camera above the side door showed her getting there at 6:57. The first one went dark at 7:11. The second one came a minute later. Why?"

"If the killer painted them before she came, then Paige might have caught the killer doing something. What? I don't know."

"And if it was after, then the killer had tracked her down and wanted to cover up his presence," she said, completing the line of reasoning.

"Right. What about the keycards? Did anyone use one to gain access to the offices after she got there?"

"We checked that. Nope. No one until the cleaning woman

found Paige's office wrecked after your call to 911."

I made a mental note. "Have they figured out what the killer hit her with?"

"A blunt object is all they can figure. Things like baseball bats and hammers leave telltale signs, but whatever the killer used here could be anything."

"I assume you spoke with the husband. Aren't they usually the most likely suspects when a married woman gets murdered?"

"That's true. A lot of that stems from spousal abuse, but we had no records of reported instances between Paige and her husband. Besides, his alibi is rock hard."

"What was he doing around the time of her murder?"

"He was loading the family van for their trip and trying to keep four kids under control at the same time."

"Oh, she had four kids? I didn't know that."

"Five, actually. The oldest goes to college at UNC Wilmington, which is where he was yesterday morning. We checked."

My heart broke for those kids and her husband. Forget the hole she left at OceanScapes and the Myrtle Beach business community. That's who would miss her the most.

"What about fingerprints?"

"That doesn't work as often as crime shows on TV let on," she said. "In this case, so many people came in and out of her office, it would be almost impossible unless we found a print so random that we had to track the person down."

"Were there any signs of a struggle? Bruises, abrasions?"

"Nope. None. Just a clean blow to the head."

"Did you find anyone between OceanScapes and the

bookstore who might have seen someone carrying a rug up the street?"

"Nope."

"I guess it would kind of stick out to see someone carrying a lumpy rug during that time of day."

"Right. They don't have cameras in their parking lots or parking garage. All they have are a few signs saying that they aren't responsible for lost or stolen possessions. Couldn't find anyone near the building either. There is a reward for anyone who has info leading to the killer."

The selfish part of me perked up at that. Extra cash is nice.

"What about a car or truck?" I said. "Anyone see the rug get dropped off?"

"Negative."

Strike two. Or three or four. I lost count. The case grew more mysterious and frustrating with each turn. Every answer seemed to bring five more questions.

Natasha appeared on the other side of the porch. She wrung her hands as her eyes darted back and forth, not settling in one place for any length of time.

"Hey, I appreciate you calling me back," I said. "Thanks for your time."

"No problem. Keep me updated if you learn anything else."

The connection ended as Natasha opened the door to the bookstore on the far end. She must not have seen me sitting here.

I followed her inside where I found her speaking to Margaret.

"Here he is." Margaret gestured to me over Natasha's shoulder.

She turned, giving me a wan smile. She thanked Margaret before turning to me. I pointed at a table in front of the coffee bar. She sat while I prepared us two cups of coffee, not knowing or caring if she wanted coffee.

I wanted to be cordial. Friendly. But I couldn't contain myself.

As soon as she swirled her coffee, set the thin red plastic stirrer on the table, and raised the paper cup to her lips, I demanded, "Why didn't you tell me you had a heated argument with Paige twelve hours before her death?"

Her eyes opened wide. Her body stiffened. She gulped.

She looked ready to run.

CHAPTER
SIXTEEN

To her credit, she didn't flee.

She took a slow sip of coffee with both hands wrapped around the cup, while her big brown eyes studied mine. Her reaction made me squirm.

Outside, a bank of puffy clouds passed in front of the sun. The bookstore grew dim. A lone patron browsed the self-help section. Margaret flipped through a Southern Living magazine at the cash register. Her shift was about over, and she was mailing in the last ten minutes. I allowed it if there was an overlap between hers and Karen's shifts, who was stocking the shelves in the kid's section.

I drummed my fingers on the wooden tabletop, waiting for an answer. The coffee tasted bitter. I'd have to adjust the grind next time. Natasha was a cool customer. I'll give her that.

"I might have fudged a little when I told you about going to Paige with the tax information," she said.

"I would call that lying."

She brushed the air with the back of her hand. "Meh, call it what you want to. I needed you to look into them and not worry about me."

"Why? Did you kill Paige?"

"That's silly. No." She melted at my glare. I didn't know I could be intimidating. She said, "Okay, let me tell you about that evening."

She explained that the person manning the desk at night prints out all the receipts of the guests departing the next morning. That way when someone comes to checkout, all the person at the desk needs to do is get their room number, pull the receipt, and hand it to them. Usually, the morning desk clerk gives them a smile, a farewell wish, and their receipt before sending them on their way.

"What if someone rents a late-night pay-per-view movie or something from the time you print the receipts to the time they check out?"

She curled a lip. "Doesn't matter. They pay with a card to the PPV service. Most visitors take the receipt and leave without studying it. They saw the fees when they checked in, so they are already familiar with the final charges. One morning, I looked at someone's receipt. I normally don't do that unless the guest asks about an extra charge. I noticed that the taxes were wrong but said nothing. The guest was happy and gone. I didn't want to make a big deal over what amounted to a few dollars."

After that, she paid closer attention and kept seeing the same thing but didn't tell anyone about it. She knew it was a big hassle to issue a refund, and doing it for a few extra dollars, she felt, wasn't worth the hassle. No one complained about the extra fraction of a percent tax fee. The thing that baffled her was that it didn't happen on everyone's bill. Another reason to keep it quiet.

"What made you finally go to Paige?" I asked.

She sipped her coffee, preparing her thoughts. "As the

months went on, these dollars were adding up. Hundreds if not thousands of dollars."

"And you thought Chris and Sabrina were keeping it for themselves?"

"Yes."

I told her about their point-of-sale system and how Sabrina had said they were still trying to get it right. "And Sabrina said she was sending out refunds."

Natasha nodded and stared out the window across the street. She seemed to be trying to reconcile this information. Sometimes the brain gets left out of the equation when a person builds up a belief in something so much that they believe it with their heart and soul. They want to hold onto their convictions when confronted with truths contrary to their views of reality.

Her gaze came back to me. "She's lying. That's what she does. She makes things up. She and Chris are evil."

The assertion didn't jibe with what I saw in my first meeting with them. "Can you prove she's lying?"

She put one hand under her chin. Four fingers on the other drummed at the table. "No. Clark, you have to believe me. Tell me you trust me?"

Her eyes pleaded with me. I knew nothing about her background except where she's from and what she does for a living. Her family, friends, and interests outside of work were a mystery. She could be a cultist or the first person at church on Sunday mornings. She could have a favorite tree at the park she likes to read under in the afternoons and be the drunkest person at the club on the weekends.

I opened my mouth to speak, but no words came out.

She pursed her lips into a tight line. "Ugh. I knew it. I

thought I could trust you to help me. First Paige didn't trust me. Now you."

She started to get up, but I grabbed her wrist and held her in place. "Wait, you didn't tell me what happened in Paige's office that night."

"I'm not sure I should now."

"Listen, you say you want me to trust you. How can I do that if I don't know the entire story?"

Her upper lip vibrated with an exhalation of air. She removed her hand from my grasp and lowered her shoulders. "Okay. When I told her what I know about the taxes, she pushed back."

"Pushed back how?"

"She questioned everything I told her."

"Did you bring proof?"

"I did. I made copies. She still questioned me."

"Was Sabrina present?"

"She was not. It was only Paige and me. Listen," she said, showing me one palm. "If I told you about our heated conversation, you would have reported me. I needed you to focus on finding evidence against Sabrina and Chris. I didn't do it."

"Can you prove that?"

"Prove what? That I didn't do it, or that one of them did?" She sipped her coffee. "I was at my apartment. I live with four roommates in a two-bedroom apartment. I share a bed with two other women from Moldova. As far as Chris and Sabrina go, no, I can't prove anything, but it exists. I'm telling you."

"What exists?"

"Proof. That's why I asked for your help."

"And you feel they did this?"

"I do."

"Okay. So why the yelling?"

"Paige was mad because I didn't come to her sooner. She said that I could lose my job over it."

"And you argued with her?"

"I did. I defended myself. I told her why it took me so long and they wouldn't know anything about it if it weren't for me. I was scared that I'd get fired and maybe have to end up going home. To Moldova."

She was shaking. From fright, anger, nervousness. I did not know. Whatever it was, it penetrated her.

I inhaled. "Look at it from Paige's perspective. Here you are coming to her out of the blue with a major accusation against two prominent employees in your company. Accusations, mind you, that could land the resort in legal hot water and the bad press that could come of it."

"Yeah, so? I had proof in black and white."

"Speaking as an employer, I would want to make sure I had all the facts that I could before moving forward. That way you're protected in case there's a simple explanation. I want to believe you, Natasha. I do, but I don't know how I can learn if they're lying. According to Sabrina, your proof only told half the story."

"I see what you're saying. I do, but they're up to something."

"Then tell me how I can figure that out."

She chewed on a fingernail. "Get into their offices. There has to be evidence."

"Even if I could, I wouldn't know what to look for."

She chewed on a different nail while bobbing her head up

and down. "I've been in Sabrina's office." She closed her eyes and lifted a hand, as though she had on a pair of virtual reality goggles. "To the left side of her desk, there's a set of filing cabinets. In the third one, there are records of refunds in the second drawer down, near the middle."

"How do you know that?"

Her eyes opened. "Because I have seen her put them in there."

"Oh, gotcha. Which office is hers?"

"It's near Chris'. There's a nameplate on her door."

"How am I supposed to sneak into her office?"

"That I don't know. I hoped you would figure something out."

Natasha must have had more confidence in me than I had in myself.

"Okay, then. I'll think about it."

"Please do," she said and placed her hand on mine.

A comforting warmth traveled up my arm. Beyond consoling hugs, I haven't had another woman touch me like this since Autumn died. It was an alien, yet somehow familiar sensation. For the first time since her death, I felt a longing I didn't think I could feel again.

"Clark," Natasha said, breaking me from my thoughts.

I looked down at our hands together on the table. They weren't intertwined. Just lying there with each other.

"Yeah, yeah," I said. "I'll think of something."

The room brightened. Whether it was because the sun emerged from the clouds or her smile, I wasn't sure.

She checked her watch. "Look, I have to go. How much do I owe you for the coffee?"

I held up a hand. "No charge. On the house."

"No, no. I insist." She stood. I rose with her. "Thank you, Clark. I know you don't need to be involved in this, but I want to see justice done for Paige."

"And you don't trust the police to do that?"

"No."

What this young woman went through to foster this distrust, I will never understand. The emotional scars she must bear.

She walked over to the counter, where Margaret put down her magazine.

"Ring her up for a small coffee, Margaret," I said.

"If you say so."

I've spoken to many people in here over the years. My general rule is, if I sit down and chat with you, coffee is on me. I enjoy meeting and talking with tourists and locals so much that it's a bonus to me to have someone to talk to. That's payment enough. I haven't charged any of these temporary friends for coffee since Autumn died. That's the reason for Margaret's hesitation.

While Natasha paid, I walked to the front of the store and stared out the windows, trying to piece the puzzle together. Again. I hadn't considered Natasha a suspect until Solomon told me about her storming out of Paige's office. The reason Natasha gave me for that confrontation was believable, but she lied to me once. She could do it again if she hadn't already. Now I had to reframe the murder scene in my head and see if Natasha fits. After learning that Paige had threatened her job, the frightening thing was, Natasha could if she had help with the body.

She came up beside me and tapped me on the arm, startling

me from my thoughts. "Hey, I have to run."

She clasped her hands behind my neck and drew me in for a hug. My heart thumped. Her perfume reminded me of lilacs. It was intoxicating.

I wrapped my hands around the small of her back, returning the hug. We parted after a few quiet moments.

"Thank you for this," she said.

"You're welcome, Natasha. I'll talk to you later."

She nodded, opened the door, and left.

I watched as she disappeared to my right. This was like a scene at the end of a book where two strangers stuck in a hostage situation shared a brief, intimate moment before departing and never seeing each other again.

"Clark! Clark! Stop her!"

Margaret ran out from behind the counter, waving something in the air.

"What?"

"Catch her! She left her debit card in the chip reader."

She reached me and handed over a card. I raced out the door to catch Natasha, but the sidewalks were empty. I ran around the side of the building in the direction Natasha was headed and didn't see any sign of her.

She was gone.

"Huh." I scratched my head.

I looked down at the card in my hand. It wasn't a credit card. It was black on the back with the magnetic strip. The front was light blue and bore her name on the bottom in gray. A white OceanScapes logo rested above that.

It was her keycard for the resort.

CHAPTER
SEVENTEEN

"It was weird, Clark," Margaret said after I returned. "I've never seen a young person have problems with that card reader before."

Since banks added the chip security measure to credit and debit cards, businesses everywhere had to adopt and install new card readers. These new readers still allowed you to swipe a card if it didn't have a chip or it couldn't read the chip. Most cards have a separate reader on the bottom of the unit for customers to insert their cards. Customers have problems sometimes, either not understanding the new process, or having a card they use so much that the chip is unreadable.

"What did she do, or not do?"

Margaret pointed at our card reader. "I gave her the total, and she put her card in it. It beeped and told her to try again. We did that a few times, then she reached into a pocket and gave me cash. Told me to keep the change. Then she hurried over to you. That's when I saw her card in there."

I held up the card and shook it. "It was all for show."

"What are you talking about?"

"She did that on purpose. She wanted me to have this."

"What is it?"

"It's a keycard to where she works."

"Well, she'll need that," Margaret said. "Do you have her number? Call her."

I did while Margaret stood there. The call went straight to voicemail. Either her phone was dead, hit "ignore", or she turned it off.

"Anyway," Margaret said, "I'm going home."

The clock on the wall showed it was past the time for Margaret to leave. She could have called Karen over to relieve her at the counter, but, knowing Margaret, she wanted to spy on me.

"Oh, I'm sorry to have kept you, Margaret."

"Doesn't bother me none. It's extra money in my pocket." An evil genius cackle followed her back to the counter where she clocked out on the computer.

Karen took over for Margaret. They were good friends outside of work. When I first hired them, they recognized each other. Both saw each other often at Travinia Italian Kitchen in Market Common for Winedown Wednesday. Which I'm sure is where they'll meet after Karen and I close the store tonight.

After shutting the door to my office, I considered what to do next. I checked the to-do list on my phone and crossed off the entries I hoped were answered.

- How was body transported?
- Where did the killer go after ditching the body?
- How many entrances are there to the executive offices?
- ~~Were the cameras painted before or after Paige arrived?~~
- Who was working in the lobby?
- What was the murder weapon?
- ~~Did anyone access the offices near the time of death?~~

The list went on.

I remembered that I had Gloria's number saved from when I set up her new phone. She might answer a few questions without caring that I'm not associated with the police.

She answered after three rings. "Ha ha, hey, Clark. What's up?"

"Can you talk right now?"

"Ooo, being real for once, are we? Is this the Clark that I know? Owns the bookstore. Tall, handsome guy?"

"Hey, I can't be a goofball all the time. This death of Paige has me curious."

"Well, if someone who's not a detective can solve a murder, it's you."

And people tell me I'm never serious about anything. Gloria is one to talk. "Yeah, right."

"No, I'm being straight with you. You're one of the smartest people I know."

My cheeks warmed. "Thanks, Gloria."

"Anyhow, I'm on my way home from work. I have a few minutes. What's on your mind?"

"I'm hoping you can fill in a few holes for me."

"Have it worked out, do we?"

"No, not yet. I can see the general outline of what happened, but I don't have enough information."

"What makes you think the police don't have everything you know?"

It was a good question, again. Except... "Natasha told me some things I'm fairly certain they don't know."

"What makes you think they wouldn't know?"

I told her about my conversation with Solomon. "Because

when I told the detective what I learned from him, she said that Natasha didn't tell her that yesterday."

"Oh, are they going to talk to her again?"

"I think they would like to but might not get the chance." I explained what happened with Natasha a few minutes ago, leaving out the part about the keycard.

"You think she might disappear?" she asked.

"Maybe. That's how it felt when she said goodbye to me."

"That Natasha is a delicate flower," she sighed. "Innocent, you know, but with an edge. She has this sweet personality, but she doesn't show a lot of emotion. She's innocent in that, even though she's been here a few years and knows the language well, sometimes there's this natural trepidation from her upbringing that makes her nervous. Over stuff that you and I would consider no big deal. She was always coming to me afraid she would get fired over some small thing and she'd get sent back, you know?"

"Can she get sent back? I thought she told me she was an American citizen."

"I don't think she can, but that doesn't keep her from being afraid that it could happen."

That was understandable, considering the current political climate. I said, "Hopefully I'm imagining things."

"Yeah, she's nervous and had an awkward goodbye. Probably had her mind on other things."

"Hope so." Time to change direction. "Who was at the desk that morning?"

"Oh, yes. My future husband, but he doesn't know it yet. Ray."

"I remember him. He was there with Natasha this morning

when I came to OceanScapes." Another item to strike off my list.

"Mmm-hmm. I like working with him."

"I'm sure you do," I laughed, recalling the handsome desk clerk.

"He's usually works the desk in the mornings, Mondays through Wednesdays," she said. "A part-timer. Goes to the Culinary Institute in Market Common in the afternoons."

"All week?"

"I think so. Monday through Friday. Boy can cook, I'll tell you that."

"I bet you'd like to have him cooking for you Monday through Friday."

There was dead air through the Bluetooth, probably imagining the handsome desk clerk as her personal chef, before a longer, "Mmm-hmm. And twice on Sundays."

"No Saturdays?"

"No, Clark. The man has to rest sometime. Maybe I'll do some cookin' for him."

"I bet you'd like that."

"No, no. I bet he'd like that."

We shared a laugh at that before I continued. "Do most people have a set schedule?"

"We do. There's not a lot of change from week to week. Kept it easy on Paige to make the schedules. It's great for us because we can plan things in advance. Like doctor's appointments and such."

The killer could have been aware who would be at the desk that morning. "Can you get me in touch with Ray?"

"Yeah, I'll text you his number when I get home. I'll tell him to expect your call. He owes me some favors."

"I understand that," I said. New hotels and resorts in Myrtle Beach have state-of-the-art security features when built, while the older ones have to keep up. That's why I had to go cheap with my security monitoring. "One last question and I'll let you go. Any idea about how to get in touch with Julieta?"

She told me, after another salacious comment about Ray which I will not repeat here.

CHAPTER
EIGHTEEN

I shot Ray a text, figuring he might be in class. Introduced myself in the message as the coffee guy in the lobby this morning, asking if I could speak with him after school. He texted back a few minutes later saying I could. Class ended around four.

After a mid-afternoon coffee, I loaded into the Jeep and drove back to the Market Common area where the Horry Georgetown Technical College campus was. Soaring loblolly pines obscured most of the college's nondescript buildings as you putter down Pampas Drive.

However, the International Culinary Institute of Myrtle Beach, tucked away on the campus, stood out. The state-of-the-art school was an architectural beauty, inside and out. Its refined lines and rotunda reminded me of a modern take on structures designed by Frank Lloyd Wright. Steel gray letters spelling CULINARY ran along its length. The landscaping and grass were impeccable.

The school operates a refined student-run restaurant and bakery along with its curriculum. I used to pop in for the farmers' markets on Thursdays for local produce and meats (and grab a pastry or two from said bakery). The school holds a variety of classes for non-students on weekends. I've been tempted to sign up for some grilling classes in their barbeque pit.

This was another place that I tried to avoid going in since Autumn's death. She loved attending the baking and cake decorating classes on weekends.

I told Ray that I could meet him at his car, that way I wouldn't need to enter the building. He said he drove an early 2000s black Honda Prelude. A friend of mine had one of those when I was in college, and I knew they could fly on the highway.

The parking lot wasn't big, and it was easy to spot his vehicle. Despite being older, his sporty little car was in pristine condition. I backed into a space a few spots down and waited. Palm fronds fluttered in the breeze, which carried the sounds of happy squeals of kids playing on the nearby Savannah's Playground. Pines swayed. The air smelled of smoking meats from the barbequing pavilion at the rear of the school.

At four o'clock, a stream of students of varying ages came through a side door together. Some spoke in knots while others went straight to checking their phones. I guess they needed to see how many Likes their latest Instagram picture or Facebook post garnered while they were in class. None, I hoped.

Ray came out by himself. His black hair was no longer spiky, but mussed. The long day and wearing a chef's hat in class tarnished its perfection. He yawned and stretched his arms over his head as droopy eyes gazed around the parking lot, perhaps looking for me.

I obliged and hopped out of the Jeep, meeting him halfway. He recognized me and we shook hands, moving off the lot and onto a spongy plot of grass to get out of the way.

"How was class?" I said.

"Oh, it was fine. Just Kitchen Fundamentals 101."

"What's that?"

"Learning the fundamentals of working in a kitchen."

"Ah. Self-explanatory."

His smile left no wonder why Gloria — and probably every other woman at OceanScapes and on this campus — was smitten with him. "No worries. No worries," he said. "It's my first semester here. Learning the ropes."

"You always wanted to be a chef?"

"I think so. When I was five years old, I used to climb on a stool to help my mama at the stove. I loved how she could create a meal from scratch."

"What kind of food did she make?"

He put a thick hand on his chest. "I'm third-generation Italian, and she had all of her mama's — my Nonna's — recipes."

"And you do too?"

"No, not all of them. Like her gravy."

"Like to go on biscuits?"

"No, no, no," he laughed. "To an Italian, 'gravy' is a homemade meat sauce. Some families keep their recipe secret. Nonna only revealed her recipe to my mother in her will."

"Daaang. That's serious."

He shrugged. "That's my family for ya. What's up? You said you wanted to ask me a few questions."

"Yeah. About yesterday."

"Man, I had to speak to the police for hours. They thought I was a suspect, bro."

"Do they still think that?"

He shrunk away.

"Sorry," I said. "Didn't mean to offend you. I have no reason to think that." I should now. He was the only person known to have been in the building at the same time as Paige that morning.

"It was crazy, man. That Detective Gomez lady and her partner put me through the ringer before another cop friend of hers looked through the surveillance footage."

"Why? What did that show?"

"That I never moved from the desk."

Could he have manipulated the feed somehow? I've seen it done in stories before. "I bet that was a relief."

"You don't know the half of it. I'm sitting there in a room with her and the other guy and she's grilling me, man. Tried to figure out a way to pin it on me. They're asking me these questions, especially the Gomez lady, and I'm like, 'Jeez, lady. I didn't do it.' I know nothing. Saw nothing."

I pictured Detective Moody berating young Ray here with a litany of grunts and snarls.

"You didn't see or hear anything?"

"Nope. Not a peep."

I wanted to scream but didn't. "I guess that answers most of my questions, then."

"Oh, okay. Sorry, bro."

"Maybe you can fill in some information for me. Some details on how you all operate."

"Why do you want to know?"

"I found her."

"You're that guy?"

"Yeah. I'm curious to know how she got there."

"Oh, word? Yeah, man. Bet that was tough. What do you want to know?"

"Thanks. I appreciate this. What's happening there during that time of the morning?"

"This time of year, it's pretty quiet. Housekeeping staff trickles in around 8:00. Checkout isn't until 10:00, so they spend a couple hours folding sheets and stocking their cleaning carts."

"How do they know which rooms to clean?"

"I print off several copies of the day's departing guests and hand it to whoever is running the crew that day. Usually Julieta."

She was next on my list of people to speak with.

"When you are up front like that at the desk, you don't know who's coming or going from the executive offices, do you?"

"Sometimes. A few of them, like Paige, Martin, and Mr. John still use the side entrance. Most prefer the elevator."

There's another entry to cross off my list. "They come in the front door like everyone else?"

"Yup. Some of them have a city parking pass. They park right out in front of the place and strut on in."

"Seems like a jerk move, taking potential prime guest spaces like that."

"Well, between me and you, some of them are jerks."

"Like whom?"

"Chris and Sabrina are the two biggest ones."

That caught my attention. "What makes you say that?"

"They like to show off and talk down to us little people. Like we're beneath their dignity or something."

"Show off how?"

"Well, Sabrina is part of the Vehicle of the Month Club. She gets a new car every few weeks and likes for everyone to see it, so she parks out on the curb every chance she gets."

"What kind of cars?"

"Usually Mercedes. Sometimes she'll drive a Tesla."

"People working in the cash office make that kind of money?"

"I don't think so," he said, and glanced over at his almost twenty-year-old car. "But if they do, I'm getting into the wrong career going here."

"Do you think she's getting money from elsewhere?"

"Dunno. Her boyfriend Chris, maybe. He's always flashing rolls of cash. Has a sweet chromed out Harley he parks in front."

Where did he get his money from? Could it be from skimming taxes? I'd add that to my list. Maybe find out over whiskey later in his office.

"Can you think of any reason someone would kill Paige?"

He stared into the clouds. "I've been asking myself the same thing, man. To us, us normal workers, she was great. Always went out of her way to help us, encourage us, and answer questions. She was as sweet as could be."

"What about her peers? Ever see any tension there?"

"Me? No. But I heard things."

"Like what?"

"Some of them didn't get along. I heard that she and Chris hated each other. Not sure why. And there was something going on with her and Martin. Whatever that was about happened recently."

"What do you mean?"

"Everything between them seemed hunky-dory until last

week."

"What happened last week?"

"Dunno. I heard there was a falling out between them over something."

"Any clue as to what?"

His lips tightened. "There's been all of this talk lately about the future of the resort. Are they selling? What's going to happen if Mr. John dies or retires? His health hasn't been great, so we're all uneasy. Everyone upstairs is tight-lipped about what's happening."

That was a new wrinkle. "How long have you been with OceanScapes?"

"Since May. Got a job there before I graduated from high school."

"That's better than my first job."

"Oh, what was that?"

"I was a bag boy at Food Lion for three months."

"Why three months?"

"I hated it. With a passion."

Ray didn't want to stand around and talk to me all night. He shifted from one foot to the other and kept glancing over at his car. I became mindful of Natasha's keycard in my back pocket.

Something pinged in the back of my brain but didn't know what. Something he said. I blinked for a second, trying to figure it out on the fly, but couldn't.

"One last thing, Ray, and I'll let you go. What can you tell me about Natasha?"

That opened a whole sordid can of worms.

CHAPTER
NINETEEN

Julieta was more difficult to reach. She did not have a phone. Gloria said the only way to get in touch with her is through Facebook Messenger. The alternative was the old-fashioned way. That is, knock on her door.

Which is where I stood, on a set of rickety wooden steps outside of a single-wide mobile home in a cramped trailer park near where they used to film the reality show Myrtle Manor. A third of the deep red paint on the stairs had peeled away. Her trailer color was that of a dingy white kitchen towel that had been through the wash fifty times after cleaning pure bacon grease out of a cast-iron skillet fifty times. The air smelled of honeysuckle. The home might have been here when Myrtle Beach was first discovered, I wasn't sure. I'd have to check Wikipedia.

They had four vehicles of various ages and states of disrepair crammed together in a tight driveway covered in gravel and sand. An assortment of kid's toys and bikes lay scattered about the small yard in between the tightly packed trailers.

From where I stood, I could almost touch a window of the neighboring trailer that looked newer, but still centuries old. I wanted to, but there was someone watching me through two slats in the blinds. I waved and turned back to the door and knocked again.

Heavy footsteps vibrated through the home, reaching the front door. It opened, revealing a heavyset woman with caramel-colored skin of Hispanic descent surrounded by more children than I could count because they kept bobbing and moving around the woman's billowy blue dress. The smell of a great Mexican restaurant hit me.

"Si, Señor?" she said.

We might have a problem here. I don't know any Spanish besides how to ask where the bathroom is. And I can't do that right. I had to take a language class during my senior year of high school to graduate. I hated the class and wasn't interested in learning another language. Back then, I didn't feel I would ever need to know either of the two languages offered, Spanish or French. It was the only class I ever made a D in.

One day in class, I asked myself if I were ever in a Spanish-speaking country, what would be an important question I might need to know to survive. I flipped through the glossary in my textbook to put together the words of the question while the teacher from Honduras droned on about conjugating verbs. She knew that I didn't care about her class and was only there to fill the graduate requirements.

Satisfied that I could now survive, I raised my hand and asked the one question that I was determined I would take with me through life.

When she called on me, I smiled and said, "Me gusto ir un baño."

She stared at me with an expression of mixed horror and

humor. The kids looked from me to her.

"What did he say?" one girl asked.

"He said that he liked to go to the bathroom."

Everyone laughed. I never learned how to ask where the bathroom was.

After that memory flashed in front of me, the woman in front of me repeated her question. "Si, Señor?"

"Hi, yes, I'm looking for Julieta. Is she here?"

The look in her eyes told me she did not understand. She opened her mouth to speak, but no words came out.

"Julieta," I said, slower. "Is she here?"

I remembered that there was a translator function on my phone. I could speak into it and it would audibly translate my question for me.

As I searched through the screens for it, one of the older girls tugged on the adult's dress and said something in Spanish. I heard "Julieta" in there somewhere. The adult looked down at the girl, and said, "Si, si."

The girl smiled at me and said in perfect English, "Mama is inside making dinner. Would you like to come in?"

* * *

I had interrupted the kids' homework session. The cadre of kids led me to the kitchen past a dining room table piled high with books, laptops, and tablets. No wonder they were so eager to see who was at the door.

Old, worn down furniture filled the living room. A man slept face down on the sofa. Another man's chin rested on his chest in a recliner. He wore a faded trucker's hat bearing the name of a local landscaping company. I admired an adult who could sleep through a hurricane. Babies can. Like the one napping in a bassinet beside the couch. An ancient television tuned to Telemundo with the volume turned down sat atop a rickety cabinet in the corner. Strips of taupe wallpaper were missing from the walls or were curled up, trying to escape their imprisonment.

A near-empty bookshelf stood against one wall. That's the detail I would notice. I didn't see a baño anywhere.

In stark contrast to the state of the home, the smells emanating from the kitchen were heavenly. No wonder these kids were chubby and happy.

They led me to the kitchen, where a plump woman in a blue dress barely tall enough to see over the counter worked in a flurry of motion. Her black ponytail was streaked with gray. Furious fingers of steam escaped from sizzling or bubbling pots and pans of various sizes on the stove. Every burner was in use.

A timer chirped on the counter. The woman stirred two pots at the same time. She took her right hand off of one wooden spoon. It traveled part of the way around the pot before coming to rest as she reached over with her now free hand and grabbed a potholder. She opened the oven door while continuing to stir another pot with her left hand and pulled out a casserole dish. She set it on a trivet on the counter before resuming to stir two pots at the same time.

My mouth hung open. The scene reminded me of Iron Chef on the Food Network. Except Julieta was doing it all by herself. There was no sous-chef in sight. Ray needed to get lessons from this woman.

I had a twenty-dollar bill in my back pocket. I considered

prepaying for a plate of whatever this was that she was preparing. Aromas of steak, rice, seasonings, and something sweet I couldn't quite place filled the air.

One of the older kids pointed me to an empty seat at the table. Whatever it was I had to ask would have to wait. They were hungry and did not want anyone to disturb Julieta. I didn't mind. It's rare to watch a master at work.

The kids resettled back into their chairs at the table and resumed their homework. The woman who answered the door disappeared.

No one paid me any attention. Like it was a normal thing to have a tall, pale stranger in the house.

I couldn't take my eyes off Julieta.

The woman who answered the door returned a few minutes later wearing her best Sunday dress and a thick, fresh coat of makeup. I didn't know if her makeover was for my benefit or if she liked to get dressed up for dinner. From the way she smiled at me, I'm guessing it was the former. She came over and instructed the children to clear the table so she could set it for dinner. I sat there the entire time and no one, besides the newly changed senorita, paid me any mind.

"La cenaestálista!" the chef proclaimed while wiping her hands on a dish towel. I didn't know what that meant. Judging from the way the men jolted from their slumbers and converged with the children in the kitchen, I figured she meant "Dinner is ready."

Then she noticed me. "Oh, hola."

"Hola," I returned, getting to my feet.

"Quiénerestú?"

"I'm sorry," I said and then pointed at my chest. "Habla no

Espanol?"

The translator girl at the door came over to Julieta and said something I couldn't understand. She looked from the girl to me and said, "Si, si."

Julieta washed her hands, and then came and shook my hand with both of hers. "You must be here to ask me about Paige," she said in clear English. "But first, dinner."

The monster in my stomach growled.

CHAPTER
TWENTY

There's a joint on 70th Avenue N. off Kings Highway named Fiesta Mexicana that, to me, serves the best Mexican food on the Grand Strand. Its bright red exterior mirrors the festive atmosphere inside. A mariachi band or a DJ plays music in a corner of one dining room, depending upon which night you are there. Drinks flow from the bar inside. The staff keep a genuine smile on their collective faces. They pass out sombreros for you to wear so you can get a memorable photo of your visit.

People go in droves for the food. Cars park at the shopping mall across the street because the Fiesta Mexicana lot is normally full. It's common to see a line of people outside the door on the patio, waiting for a table.

The menu, mostly, is what you would find in most other such establishments. One thing Autumn and I loved was the Fiesta Mexicana Special. The menu says it serves two, but we could get at least one dinner and two lunches at home out of it. They serve it on a plate piled high with tender grilled slices of steak, chicken, shrimp, and homemade chorizo with onions and peppers served with Mexican rice, beans, fiesta salad and tortillas.

What Julieta placed on the table before us reminded me of

that, but better.

"What is this?"

"Bandeja Paisa," she said.

"What's that?"

"It's a meal that my family made for the farmers in the mornings to get them full of protein for work during the day."

"Where was this?"

"Columbia."

I gestured to the food on the table. "And what am I looking at here?"

The little girl who spoke English pointed and explained that there were two types of Colombian sausage, ground beef, rice, red beans, chicharrónes, an arepa, a plantain, a slice of avocado—you know, to be healthy—and a fried egg to top it all off.

"So, we're having breakfast for supper?"

A smile of recognition spread across Julieta's face. "Si, si senor."

Half an hour later, after we devoured dinner, laughed, and had an all-around fun time, the children cleared the dishes and were cleaning up for Julieta in the kitchen while us adults removed ourselves to a cramped deck out back. One man handed me a Negra Modelo. We clinked bottles, and they offered me a seat in a blue plastic Adirondack chair in the corner beside a small, covered grill.

I wasn't comfortable bringing up the discussion of Paige to Julieta in front of everyone. We did not discuss the topic at the dinner table.

"Look, Mr. Thomas," Julieta said over a glass of red wine. "We all know why you are here. We can discuss it while the niños are inside."

"Should we do this in private?" I said, glancing at the three men and one woman clustered together.

"No, no. It's fine. I've already told them everything several times over. There's nothing I can tell you they don't already know."

I held up a hand. "Okay. If you say so. If something comes up that you don't feel comfortable saying around them, let me know, and we'll step around the corner."

She thought about it. "Si. What would you like to know?"

I had come up with a mental list of questions to ask on the way over. I should have written them down or dictated them into my phone because I'd already forgotten about half of them. Rookie mistake.

"About what time did you enter Paige's office?"

"A little after eight," she answered. "I got there early and gathered cleaning supplies for my cart before going upstairs to clock in."

"Isn't that working off the clock?"

She shrugged. "I suppose. Their offices are the first places I clean. The sanitation closet is downstairs near the service garage. It saves time for me to get my cart loaded and take it upstairs with me when I clock in. I don't mind."

Makes sense. She's losing some money doing it that way, but I admired the work ethic. If I found out one of my employees was working off the clock that way, I would adjust their pay and give them a minor scolding. Julieta getting there at that time meant that less than an hour passed between me finding the body and her going into Paige's office.

"What did you see when you entered?"

Julieta squeezed her eyes shut and pursed her lips. She reopened them and said, "It was chaos, Mr. Thomas." She said it like Meester. "Her office is normally neat. Orderly. This time, there were papers thrown everywhere."

"What papers?"

"I'm not sure. Just normal sized papers and the timecards."

"What else did you see?"

"Her chair was overturned. The desk was out of place. Like it had been shoved aside in a fight. The rug was missing."

Gomez didn't mention any signs of a struggle. Could the desk have moved while the killer was rolling her into the rug? I tried to envision her getting hit on the back of the head and falling forward or to the side. Maybe she was sitting at her desk and her weight shoved the desk off kilter.

"Would whoever killed her needed to move the desk to roll her up in the rug?"

"No. It's a large office. She has a desk on one end and shelving behind it that holds some of her awards and business supplies. The rug sat under a seating area with four chairs and a coffee table on the other. I think her and other important people would have informal meetings there."

"I assume all of that was messed up too?"

"Yes."

"Did you see any blood?"

"Yes, I had to clean it." She shivered.

"Where was it?"

"Behind where her office chair and on the corner of her desk."

"Hmm. Notice anything out of place? Besides the obvious."

"No, I didn't, but then again, I was focused on the area I had to clean."

"Isn't her office at the end of the hall?"

"Si."

"When you get off the elevator, what direction do you turn to get to her office?"

"Left. Hers is the last door on the left. Her office is next to Mr. McInally's."

Interesting. "Do you know much about the people who work in those offices?"

"I don't. I try to finish before they come."

"What do you do after you clean the offices?"

"I go across the street and help clean rooms."

"What time do you get off work?"

"By three, if we can. Check-in starts at four in the afternoon, and they want all rooms ready before then. It's not so difficult to do this time of year. During the summer, whoo boy," she said and took a long, comforting drink of wine.

"Any idea who might have done this?"

"No." Her eyes widened. "Miss Paige was the nicest woman. I don't know how she was to other people, but to me and our staff, she was always courteous."

"Can you tell me about that? Do you work directly for OceanScapes?"

"No, I get my paychecks from Sani-Queen. They are a staffing service for custodial workers."

"Do you know why OceanScapes outsources that instead of doing the hiring themselves?"

"I don't know for sure. I think with the seasonal movement of the hotel staff, Paige wanted to have a portion of the workers where there was little paperwork. Let someone else deal with the hiring and firing."

"What happens if one of you does something wrong or is underperforming?"

"They call Sani-Queen and tell them to take care of it."

"Do they? Take care of it, that is."

"Yes, with swiftness."

"Is there much staff turnover among you?"

"With our crew assigned to OceanScapes, no. Most of us have been together for years."

"How many are you?"

She looked at the sky and counted to herself. "There are four of us housekeepers. Maria, Sandra, Martha, and myself. Sandra is part-time. There's a full-time janitor and a part-time janitor, James and Willie."

"I met James."

She took another sip of wine. "Oh, that James. He sure is a character."

"Is he the full-timer or part-timer?"

"Full-time, but I'm not sure how."

"What do you mean?"

Julieta batted a chubby hand. "Oh, he's a clown. Thinks he's a stand-up comedian. I think he does the amateur hours at local bars for comedy."

"Is he funny?"

"Meh," she wiggled a hand. "He can be. Loves his cards too."

"Cards?"

"Yes, he loves the poker."

One man perked up with a smile and raised his bottle. "Poker! Si, si."

Julieta held a hand against the side of her mouth. "Ricardo here doesn't speak much English, but he understands beer, liquor, and poker."

"Ah, the Universal Language," I said.

"Yes, you get it. James comes over and plays cards about once a month with the guys here."

"What did you mean when you said that you're not sure how James is full-time?"

"Oh, Willie will come in and do his work when he's not scheduled after James stayed out at a club half the night."

"Does Sani-Queen know about this?"

"I do not know."

"Are all of you with Sani-Queen tight-knit? Those of you who work at OceanScapes?"

"Mostly. Sandra has a sick mother and infant she has to care for. That is why she works part-time. She doesn't have much free time outside of the home. James and Willie are cousins."

Outsourcing a janitorial staff was an unfamiliar concept. I had no use for it with my business but could understand how some bigger motels along the strip could.

We were quiet for a minute while we worked on our drinks. I downed my beer and placed the empty bottle on a wicker side table. The action allowed me to sort my thoughts, and I concluded that there wasn't much more for me to ask of Julieta.

As I drove away from the cramped trailer park, it occurred to me that Julieta didn't have anything useful to say that might point me in the killer's direction. Was there something she didn't say that might be of use?

CHAPTER
TWENTY-ONE

I needed a shower after listening to what Ray told me about Natasha. Doing that wasn't an option after leaving the Culinary Institute, so I drove to the house after the early dinner with Julieta and her family. Chris had told me to swing by OceanScapes after seven, so I had an opening. Karen would shut down the store.

As the hot water cascaded over me, various scenarios for Paige's death played out in my head. People I spoke with at OceanScapes suggested a rift between Paige and Chris. Could a business disagreement give him the motivation to kill her? He was a relative newcomer to OceanScapes while Paige had been there from the literal ground up. It sounded like she was one of the key people in the entire place. The only way to remove her without her voluntarily stepping away would be death.

The term "Over my dead body" sprang to mind.

Chris, apparently, was there to help grow the business and expand to other cities. How did he go from prison to such a prominent role within that organization? Did he buy-in, or know somebody? What were his qualifications?

He had access to the offices. Julieta said his office was next to Paige's. There's the opportunity part of the equation. He could have hit her with anything. There are means. But motive? I haven't gotten there. Yet.

Ray mentioned animosity between Paige and Martin, the VP. He didn't know what it was about. Whatever the reason, something happened recently to cause it. Another avenue to investigate.

The apparent disappearance of Natasha troubled me. When she vamoosed, I wondered why. She said she was at home with her roommates around the time Paige was murdered. They could vouch for her. Allegedly. Maybe she made the roommate thing up to throw me off the trail. She talked about how important Paige was to her. I couldn't see a motive.

Then I talked to Ray, and that all changed. She instantly jumped to the top of the suspect list. Then why did she slip me her keycard? What did she want me to find? It had to be something with Chris and Sabrina.

Who else? There were threats from the oil companies. I only had a passing knowledge of that industry. I only thought about it as far as being able to go gas up my Jeep. Most of that comes from the Middle East, Texas, and the Gulf of Mexico, I thought. I could see some shady stuff there. Who were the people wanting to drill off the coast? Maybe the reporter girl, Erica Sullivan, would know.

There's three. It couldn't have been Paige's husband. He was at home during the time of her death, loading up for a vacation with the kids that will never happen. He's out. Thankfully.

Perhaps another suspect would appear.

I do my best thinking in the shower and in the car. I'm not sure why. It's always been that way. The idea for the bookstore sprang from a shower session. Car rides and showers were a great cure for writer's block. The publisher gives me detailed plot outlines when I get a ghost-writing gig. Usually, they lay out most of the story. There are still times when I write myself into a corner and have to figure out how to get out of it. It doesn't work if I pressure myself. There's something about the mindless task of driving or washing that allows the brain to flow better. I was hoping this shower would be fruitful. So far, nothing. Probably because I'm over-thinking it.

I finished rinsing the soap out of my hair and grabbed the Irish Spring body wash. I'm way overdue for a haircut. It's getting long. And a trip to the gym. I looked down at my pudgy self. The flab wasn't there before Autumn died. I have never been an exercise rat, but we loved riding our bikes around Surfside and going for long walks on the beach. Cliché, I know, but it was the life we led. We spent as much time outside as we did inside. We loved to eat, but we worked it off one way or the other.

After turning off the water and wrapping a towel around myself, I stood in front of the dresser. There is a picture of us on top of it in a silver frame that never fails to make me smile. We took a trip to Destin, Florida a few years before her passing, and it became our favorite vacation destination thereafter. It was love at first sight.

We had found a washed-up log on the white sand beach, sitting halfway between the tide and sand dunes. The sun was on its descent, casting the beach in soft tones of orange and yellow. Autumn was wearing a black sun dress and flip flops. She sat on the log, raking the toes of her left foot in the sand, and put her right leg up on the log. I got out my camera and started taking pictures. She put a hand over her right knee, looked up at the sky, and then at me with a look I will never forget. It was a mixture of contentedness, happiness, and desire.

And I captured that exact moment in this photo. In the two years since her death, I have sadly and reluctantly removed all other photos of her from our home. There were pictures of her in every room. A constant reminder of our lives together. It became too much. Too depressing. But this one picture, this beautiful, joyous, sexy picture, I could not part with.

I had to let her go. She would want me to move on with my life. I had to remind myself that every day. But still...

In two years, I haven't thought of being with another woman. Her death was too sudden. She was so young. It never seemed right. It never felt right.

The dark memory of the night of her death will haunt me for the rest of my life. Autumn was a clerk at the courthouse and often worked overtime to finish filing documents. She was the Clerk of the Court for the Chief Municipal Judge of the City of Myrtle Beach, Judy Whitley. They handled motor vehicle offenses (drunk drivers, parking tickets, etc.), trespassers, shoplifters, and property disputes. Because of the area, they heard a lot of cases regarding boating violations and broken fishing laws.

When she didn't return home one night, I called down there on an afterhours number not available to the public. A night security guard answered and told me he'd go check on her.

He found her in her office with her head down on her desk. He thought she was sleeping. She wasn't.

She died of a sudden, massive heart attack at her desk at the courthouse.

Autumn had an irregular heartbeat. She was diagnosed with the arrhythmia as a child. She took medication to keep it at bay, but something happened that evening that caused her heart to fail. We knew it might happen, but she had to live her life as though it weren't a possibility. Better to live freely than under a blanket of fear.

I reached out and touched the picture and breathed for a few seconds.

Then it hit me deep down. I didn't want to admit it, but it's true. I'm looking into Paige's death because of Autumn.

I understood what Paige's husband was going through. The anguish, the physical and mental pain, the sudden loss. Yes, I lost Autumn in a different manner, but the situation was similar.

I threw on a short-sleeved Hawaiian shirt with brightly colored palm fronds and red parrots arrayed on the fabric, along with a pair of khaki golf shorts for the occasion. This was about as dressy as I got.

I don't wear a watch. I only wear long pants when the temperature dips below fifty degrees. Sometimes not even then. Flip-flops were my footwear of choice. About the only times I wear closed-toe shoes is when I play golf.

A short time later, I entered OceanScapes. Chris met me in the lobby.

We shook hands, and he guided me down the hallway to the employee elevator. It sat in the middle of the building. He slid his keycard into a slot on the call button panel next to the elevator doors. The little LED light turned from red to green. I spied the set of stairs at the end of another hallway to my right as the elevator doors opened.

"After you," Chris said.

"Thanks," I mumbled and entered the elevator.

Besides the standard options on the call button panel in case of emergencies or wanting to close the door quickly if an annoying coworker was rushing to get in, the options of where the elevator could go were for the lobby, basement, and second floor.

He hit the "2" when the doors slid shut. The car jolted as it rose.

"How's your day been so far?" he asked. "Still looking into what happened to Paige?"

"A little," I said, not quite truthfully. "I spoke to a couple people, went home and cleaned up before coming back here."

"Aww, you didn't have to do that for me," he laughed.

I smiled. "Meh, I didn't have time this morning before I left the house, and I felt like I was stinkin'. Didn't want you to have to fumigate your office after I left."

He laughed again as the doors slid open, guiding me to the left upon exiting. From the way the downstairs staff talked about the executive offices, I figured the halls would be gilded with gold, and they would walk on polished marble floors as befitting someone of their stature.

That couldn't be further from the truth. The walls were the same light blue as downstairs. Black and white tile flooring ran the length of the hallway. There was an alcove opposite the elevator harboring a kitchenette in need of updating. The time clock was on the wall to the left of the alcove, flanked by two racks of timecards. A fluorescent light here and there needed changing. It was kind of basic, if not disappointing. I expected more.

I glanced to my right as I left the car and saw Sabrina

walking out of one office and into another. She waved. Her face was a mask of concentration. I counted six doors down that way.

"It's about quitting time for her," Chris said. "She's wrapping up for the day."

I said nothing and followed him down the hall past two doors on opposite sides of the hall. Six more doors lined the hall on this side of the elevator. Twelve in total. One had to be a conference room. Another was for Sabrina's cash office.

He led me to middle of the three doors on the left side. The door at the end, next to Chris', had yellow police tape strung across it. Must be Paige's office. A large aerial photo of the resort being built, and several "Best of the Beach" plaques dominated the wall opposite her door. A door to the stairs was at the end of the hall. It looked like I needed no keycard to access those.

A security camera set in the upper corner of the wall at the top of the stairs still had black spray paint over it. Dark mist was on the walls to the side of it, like a permanent shadow. Until it gets repainted, that is.

"They said it might be a day or two before we can get back into Paige's office," he said, sliding his keycard into a slot above the doorknob.

"Is there any hurry?"

He shook his head. "No, none of us want to go in there. She has things in her filing cabinet and on her computer we'll need. We'll have to at some point."

I wondered what else a person might find in her office as we entered his.

CHAPTER
TWENTY-TWO

"Have a seat," Chris said, pointing to a seating group comprising three leather club chairs and a white coffee table made of driftwood with a glass top.

I paused, struck by a familiar sight.

"What is it?" Chris said, noticing my hesitation.

"The rug," I said.

"What about it?"

"Is that the same one I found Paige wrapped up in yesterday?"

He stared at the floor. "Probably. All of our offices, except for Mr. John's, are decorated identically to each other."

"Okay, okay. Cool," I said. His desk and office chair matched the style of the sitting group, as did a row of bookshelves lining the wall behind it. The middle unit had a two-door cabinet under two shelves containing several trophies and awards. I have something similar in my office at the store, minus the honorifics. A long, narrow window let in sunlight in the space between the shelves and the ceiling. Two tall file cabinets stood on the left side of the room. A curio cabinet sat in one corner, filled with what looked like various motorcycle figurines.

A "brag wall" above the file cabinets had two framed degrees. One from Coastal Carolina, the other from The Yale School of Management. Interesting. Another brushed nickel frame held a newspaper article with a picture of Chris. At least the picture wasn't a mugshot. He was wearing a blue suit with a red tie. The headline read: *FROM JUVENILE HALL TO THE DEAN'S LIST*. That explained the whole prison thing, I hoped. I wasn't sure how old the article was, but the Chris in the picture was a good deal younger than the Chris currently pouring whiskey from a glass bottle. The label read "Belle Meade."

"Neat or on the rocks?" he asked.

"Neat, thank you."

I settled into a club chair facing his desk as he handed me a glass containing the amber liquid. I tilted the glass this way and that, causing the whiskey to slosh around the tapered sides of the glass.

"Is this one of those Glencairn glasses?" I asked. It was stylish as far as whiskey glasses are concerned. A tulip-shaped bowl sat atop a tapered pedestal. It fit into my hand well.

"It is. Its shape is supposed to reveal the depth and nuance of whiskey while enhancing the aroma of the spirits it contains."

I studied the glass and sniffed. The Belle Meade smelled strong enough, but I couldn't tell if it was because of the glass. The scent suggested smoothness. Right up my alley.

"To be honest," he said, "I can't tell any difference. Bought this set in Scotland at a local distillery when I went back to visit family a few years ago. A nice memento of the trip."

He sat. We clinked glasses. A few drops of bourbon splashed out of his glass onto the rug. He didn't seem to notice.

We took our first sips in unison. He looked like a practiced professional. I winced a smidge as the liquor hit the back of my throat.

"You know, I've always favored Scottish whiskey. But I've learned to appreciate Kentucky bourbon." He took another drink and smacked his lips. "It's my Americanization."

We chatted about business and life on the Boardwalk.

"I remember that they were working on it when I first got here a couple years ago," Chris said. "I never visited here before I got this job.

"Yeah. The city spent a lot of money to revitalize the Boardwalk. They wanted to focus on it first because that's the tourist draw. They got the oceanfront and Ocean Boulevard updated but held off on bringing the areas three blocks back into the twenty-first century."

He took a meditative sip from his glass. "I didn't know what went on in the Downtown Development meetings until last night. Mr. John told me to go in Martin's place because of Paige, so I went. Most of my dealings here revolve around areas outside of Myrtle Beach."

"What is it you do?"

"Mr. John hired me a couple years ago as a business consultant because he was interested in opening up other OceanScapes resorts. I had success before in helping restaurants expand their footprint."

That explained Natasha saying that Chris didn't do much about the business here in Myrtle Beach and seemed to travel frequently.

"Wait, you're looking to expand?"

"Of course. Business it good. Mr. John is looking to the future of the company when he's gone."

"Someone told me they saw people in here inspecting the resort because they thought he was going to sell?"

Chris laughed. "Sell? Nah. He probably saw the architect and his team. They've been here a couple times inspecting the place to get an idea of what we want in future designs."

"How did you know they were hiring for your job?"

"LinkedIn," he said, referring to the online business networking website. "I wasn't really looking for a job, but I saw the listing and thought it was time to move South."

"Like half the permanent population here."

He snorted. "Yep. It didn't take me long to figure that out. A lot of New England money in Myrtle Beach."

"I thought that business consultants worked for themselves or as part of a larger consulting firm?"

"Yeah. I worked for a group based in Boston before this. Many of your big companies like Google, IBM, Samsung, Volkswagen, and Disney all formed their own in-house consulting groups in recent years."

"Hmm," I said, taking a sip of whiskey. "That'd save money, wouldn't it?"

"Definitely. By focusing on one company, in-house consultants have several advantages over external firms, like having a company-wide perspective, higher levels of confidentiality, and it makes it easier to roll out new initiatives. Mr. John was ahead of the curve on this one."

"Sounds like it. Where all are you looking to expand?"

He took a drink. "Now, I'm not supposed to say. This isn't public knowledge."

"Your secret is safe with me. I don't have any friends in the corporate espionage game."

"Three places at present," he said, ticking them off on the fingers on his left hand. "Hilton Head, Tybee Island, and Amelia Island in Florida."

"Popular spots. Close enough that those familiar with the OceanScapes name might be interested in checking out your other resorts."

He fired a finger gun at me. "Bingo. That's what we're banking on. We have some hot prospective properties in all three I've been scoping out. Particularly one on Amelia Island."

"Cool."

"That one's a little farther than a quick drive, so I charter a flight at the airport and fly down to the Fernandina Beach Municipal Airport. It's a quick trip."

"Interesting. I heard something else too that might go against everyone thinking you might sell."

"Oh, what's that?"

"That they're not sure what's going to happen to the business with Mr. John."

"What about Mr. John?"

"He's getting older and there doesn't seem to be a plan for what happens if he retires or passes away."

He grimaced. "Oh, that? That's been settled."

That was newsworthy. "What's going to happen?"

"Look, this isn't public either, but with Paige's death, it's bound to come out."

"What does Paige have to do with the future of the business?"

"That's it, mate. She was the future of the business."

"I don't get it." Among many other things.

"We had a meeting two weeks ago with the ownership

group and us executives where Mr. John announced his impending retirement and what would happen if he dies before then. He named Paige as his successor."

I almost spit out the bourbon in my mouth. "What? I thought she did H.R.?"

"No, no, mate." He wiped a tear from his eye. "Paige was much more than that. She was our motivator, our shoulder to cry on, the voice of reason, you name it. She had her hands in everything. It's the way it was. She had an all-encompassing vision for the company that none of the rest of us had. Not even Martin."

"What about Martin? He's the Vice President, right? I figured he'd be next in line."

"So did we. But when Mr. John laid out his reasons for selecting Paige, we all saw his vision and realized she was the right person to move us forward."

"What did Martin think about it?"

"He was devastated, mate. When Mr. John said Paige's name at that podium, everyone looked at her for her reaction. She didn't know until that moment. Neither did Martin. He paled and stormed out of the room."

"Oh, man."

"Yeah. We're in full scramble mode now."

"So now will Martin get the call?"

"Yeah, probably. If he still wants it." He crossed his legs and drained the last of the Belle Meade. "Now tell me about your business. How did Myrtle Beach Reads come about?"

Without thinking about it, I finished my glass. Chris reached for the bottle on the table and refilled our glasses. I didn't intend to have over two fingers of alcohol, but the origin of my bookstore dredged up memories I needed a little liquid courage to get through. My goal was to get him talking. If that meant that I had to go to a dark place to do so, then so be it. Hopefully, I could remember this conversation in the morning.

The warmth from the first glass coursed through me. I'm not a bourbon connoisseur by any stretch of the imagination, but this was among the best I've had. Ever.

"My wife loved books. Always carried a book with her. Had a never-ending stack to be read on her nightstand. No matter how many she read, she'd get more from the library, or Walmart, Barnes and Noble, Books-a-Million, Amazon, the grocery store, gas station, you name it. She was always looking for her next read."

"A bookworm?"

"Oh yes. She couldn't bear to part with her books. She jammed the attic with boxes of them. Closets filled."

"What did you think about that?"

"Meh. It wasn't a problem. We had had a big house. It was her joy. We'd face the problem when it became too much. She was a sensible person. I was sure she would have gotten rid of them if it became too much."

He pointed a crooked finger at me and twirled it. "You keep talking about your wife in the past tense. Divorced?"

I pursed my lips. "Nope. Dead."

"Oh, mate," he said. "I'm so sorry. How long has it been?"

"About two years. She died of a sudden heart attack while working late at her desk one night."

"How old was she?"

"Forty-two."

"How old are you?"

"I'm forty now. Thirty-eight when she died."

"I didn't think you were much younger than me. That must have been horrible. I feel for you."

"It was. It was. She kept her job at the courthouse while I ran the bookstore. But she helped where she could. It was her dream to run a bookstore. I'd worked retail for about a decade when she had the idea for us to open one. I had worked for Target as a jack-of-all-trades district trainer and I knew all about merchandising, backroom inventory, and the ins and outs of receiving. I was in management and learned about hiring and firing and how to open and close a store."

"Where did you get the resources to open it?"

"She had a wealthy grandfather from New Jersey who died. He owned a factory that makes circuit boards for stop lights. He left her a lot of money in his will, as he did for the rest of his grandkids."

"Bet he made a killing off government contracts."

"Oh yes. Shipped them all over the United States. We took that money and started the business debt-free."

"Good for you. Sucks for her grandpa, though."

I waved a hand. "Nah. Guy was in his nineties and lived a full life. Traveled all over the world. Had five wives."

"And he still had money left over for the grandkids?"

"Yup. Started a trust for the kids under 18 years old."

"Big money. What about you? Does owning the bookstore dredge up old memories of your wife?"

"Every day," I nodded. "When we designed the interior of the store, our brand, I laid out where and how the books would be presented by section. She did all the decorating. I haven't touched a thing since she passed. She had a great eye for mixing nautical and bookish motifs I don't possess."

"I'll come by and check it out," Chris said, draining the last of his second glass. "What about business? Is it good?"

I smiled. "Oh, yeah. I get busier every year. More new people come to Myrtle Beach every year, while the same people keep coming back. Many have become regular, albeit yearly, customers, but they keep coming and tell their friends. I don't even do much advertising, to tell the truth. I used to put coupons in those travel brochures you see all over the place, but I pulled out a couple years ago and didn't see a drop in business."

"Saved you some money."

"While earning more and more." I sipped my whiskey while Chris refilled his glass. He offered to fill mine, but I declined. Maybe later. I thought about why Natasha originally came to me. The suggested tax-skimming. I understood where Chris might have a weakness to put more cash in his pocket on the downlow. Sabrina had a logical explanation about what was happening with the accommodations' taxes, but that didn't mean that they were returning all the money to each guest who had been overcharged. Did it?

"So business is good? Awesome. Have you thought about expanding?"

I took a long sip to collect my thoughts. "It was something we discussed before she died. There aren't many small bookstores like ours in the area. We might if we expanded to different markets, but I haven't given it much thought in two years."

"I'm not too familiar with the book scene. I mostly read books on my iPad."

"There's a strike against you. Bet you get them all from Amazon?"

"Guilty," Chris said, raising a hand.

How many times had he made that plea?

CHAPTER
TWENTY-THREE

I forced a laugh. "I won't hold it against you."

"I could help you with it," he said.

"Help with what? Buying actual books from my store?"

"No," he said. "Well, yeah sure. But I was talking about expansion. It's what I do, man. It's in my blood. Yeah, you'd want to change the name, but I think one thing that helps you in your marketing is the name. Or style of name, that is."

"I don't follow you."

"It can by hyperlocal. Myrtle Beach Reads can just as easily be Surfside Beach Reads, Wrightsville Beach Reads, Cocoa Beach Reads, South Beach Reads. Keep your branding and your style but do it in a way that you can integrate with the quaint small shops prevalent in coastal destinations."

A tingle ran through my veins. It might have been from the Belle Meade or what he said.

"It would be easy marketing, too," he continued. "That name has the almost perfect keywords for Google searches. You get someone planning to go somewhere, like here, and they know they're going to want to check out a local bookstore, what are they going to search for?"

"Bookstores in Myrtle Beach. Yeah, I've had many people

say that's how they discovered me."

"I bet you pop up at the top of the list."

"Not quite at the top, but under Barnes & Noble and Books-A-Million. The big box bookstores."

"Right, but places like those don't capture the essence of a coastal book shop."

"Small, independent bookstores like mine are making a comeback."

"See? When people come on vacation, they want the beach experience. Sure, you're going to have your sheep who go to those bigger places because that's what's familiar to them, but others will aim for places like yours so they can feel like it's part of the adventure."

"How would you help me?"

"Let me think on it. I'll jot down a few ideas. Come visit your store. And we'll sit down again."

"Sounds like a plan."

He pointed the pinky finger on the hand holding his glass at me. "But you didn't come to talk business, did you?"

Now it was my turn. "Guilty as charged."

"Go ahead. Shoot. I can't promise I can answer every question because of the police investigation, but I'll fill in details where I can.

"The number one question is why would anyone want to kill Paige? She was a customer at my store and always seemed pleasant. From what everyone has told me, she cared about her employees."

He put a hand to his forehead and brushed his hair back. I think I saw some blobs of hair grease go flying, but that might have been my imagination. "No, she was a sweetheart with the employees. Universally adored. She gave many people a chance here. She oftentimes wouldn't hire the person with the most experience, but one who might have been in a hard place in their lives. Like they showed her something in the interviews that informed her that this person was the right fit. She had the knack of hiring the right person at the right place at the right time."

"An excellent judge of character then?"

"Oh, yes. You had to be in her position. I've worked for several other companies with huge HR departments. I've been around many human resource directors, but Paige was the best. I mean, the absolute best. She's why OceanScapes was so well run."

I wondered how her loss would affect the type of person who worked here going forward. Would the resort go downhill?

"So, none of the employees?"

He looked away. Took a sip. Looked back. "No, Clark. None that I can think of."

"Could it have been the oil people?"

He shot a finger gun at me. "That's who jumped to mind first. I don't know all the details. I know she received some nasty emails over the years after she began fighting against the offshore drilling."

"Do you know of any specific oil companies that might have targeted her?"

"None that I can think of. Then again, that's not my field. I never was a part of her dealings with the causes. Nor any causes to tell the truth."

"Anyone else?"

He stuck out his lower lip. "No, none that I can think of."

"What about Martin? He got passed over for Paige. You said he was furious."

"I guess so. Still is. Or was upset, I'll admit. I'm not going to lie and say he didn't cross my mind."

I can't imagine Mr. John would approve of everything Chris was telling me this evening. All of this, I would think, would be proprietary information. Did he have an angle?

"I agree. Let me ask a few questions about her position if you don't mind?"

"I'll help where I can. I didn't know much about her job, though."

"No problem. So, Sabrina is going to handle Paige's role for a bit?"

"Yeah. At least with the payroll."

"Do you think she will take over Paige's job? Would that be a big promotion?"

He shifted in his seat, crossing and recrossing his legs. "It would. I'm not sure she wants it, though."

"Why wouldn't she?"

"Yeah, the money's better, but she'd have to work a lot more. Paige was here at all hours. Sabrina's current position has a set schedule. She knows that at seven-thirty, she's clocking out for the day, and she'll be off every weekend."

Or, she can stay in the cash office and skim money off of people's bills. I didn't say that out loud. I liked having teeth, of which I surely would have lost one or two when Chris would have punched me. In theory. Speaking of punching: "So, Sabrina punches a time clock?"

"Yep."

"How did she get chosen to take over for Paige? At least

temporarily?"

"Sabrina helped Paige with the payroll when she went on maternity leave, so she got the call to do it this week. People still need to get paid. You know? She was having a hard time with it this afternoon."

"Why is that?"

"Something about the timecards not jiving. Usually the cards are in slots on either side of the time clock. All neat and orderly. But they were everywhere in her office. Like a hurricane had been through there. She had to spend a couple hours sorting them out before she could even get to putting them into the computer."

"Seems old-fashioned to me. These time cards."

"I agree. The new places will be digital. Mr. John, for some reason, hasn't wanted to upgrade here. It's a head-scratcher. Guy has all the money in the world but wants to be a cheapskate about it."

Odd. "My employees' clock in and out on the computer up front."

He glanced at the thick, silver watch on his wrist. "What else ya got? I have to meet someone down on the Marsh Walk for dinner in a few."

There were several questions remaining I wanted to ask. I figured I had time for one more question. After sorting through my thoughts and theories, one question stood above the rest. "What can you tell me about Natasha?"

"Natasha?" His brow furrowed and a brief, revealing smile showed that I'm sure he meant to keep hidden. "You mean the desk clerk?"

Natasha wasn't just any "desk clerk" according to Ray.

"Yes, her."

"I don't know much. I don't come in much contact with the hourly workers here."

If what Ray told me was true, then Chris came into a lot more contact with Natasha than he let on. Like, a lot more contact. I didn't figure I could verify Ray's story with Chris. I doubt that he would come right out and admit it.

"Well, what can you tell me?"

"She seems like a good worker. I pass her on my way in and out of the lobby most days."

"Do you go in through the lobby or come up the stairs?"

"The lobby, mostly. I usually park out front and it's shorter to get from Point A to Point B by cutting through there. If I wanted to use the side entrance, I'd have to walk around the building. I still haven't adapted to your Southern summers with the stickiness and heat. I'd rather stay in air conditioning as much as I can."

"I hear you ride a Harley. Are they air conditioned?" I asked, knowing the obvious answer.

"You got me there," he smiled. "I sacrifice comfort to enjoy my Harley. But, yes, I do see Natasha in my comings and goings. I mean, how could you not notice a beautiful creature like that?"

The memory of that hug and her pressing herself up against me brought an array of guilty thoughts. Then she disappeared.

"In talking to the employees here, I learned a couple things about her."

"Like what?"

"First, that she's a good worker."

"Seems like that to me. Sabrina talks about her sometimes.

She told me that Natasha is ambitious and wants to move up in the company."

"Interesting." Maybe she wanted Sabrina's job? "Second, she got into some sort of argument with Paige the night before her death."

"Yes, I know about that. Sabrina told me that Paige called her into the office after Natasha revealed her suspicions about Sabrina, and somehow me, have been taking a cut of the hospitality taxes."

Sabrina didn't tell me about this. Solomon didn't mention Sabrina either. Maybe he didn't know she was in the office with Paige and Natasha. "Do you know what came of it?"

"Paige told Sabrina that Natasha stormed out. I'm not clear why specifically. Might have been because Paige didn't believe her and said she'd have to check into it. The thing about Natasha is that she has this Russian fatalism streak to her. You know? What is to be will be."

For someone who said he didn't know much about Natasha, knowing that character trait, I think, would be difficult to glean from walking past her in the lobby. Which led me to the new factoid I've learned. I sipped whiskey before continuing. "Okay. Third, she gets around."

"What do you mean?" he said, shifting uncomfortably in his seat. Chris might be slick and Ivy League educated, but one thing he was not was a poker player.

"That she sleeps with a lot of the employees here."

His mouth opened and closed twice before he muttered. "Hmm. That's interesting. Where did you hear that?"

Revealing Ray here would surely lead to his firing. "I'm not here to reveal my sources. But from your response, I'm going to gather that it's true."

He sat back, uncrossed his legs, smoothed the creases from his trousers, and flexed his prodigious biceps. "Look, I don't know what you've been told, but I would tread carefully."

That's all I needed. Ray told me that there was a rumor that Natasha and Chris knocked boots a couple times and their relationship ended in a mess. Then Chris jumped to Sabrina. Perhaps part of the reason Natasha came to me was to get back at the two of them.

"Could Natasha's squabble with Paige have also been about improper relationships with coworkers?"

He looked away. "I don't know. Sabrina didn't mention that."

He was hiding something.

He checked his watch again. "Look, Clark, I really gotta run. We'll circle back to how I can help you expand one day later this week, okay?"

"Sounds good," I said. The hair on the back of my neck stood on end as the thrill of possible expansion of the business settled in. Then, as I stood to leave, I saw something that caused me to hesitate. I almost said something but held off. I liked having teeth, remember?

I needed to come back without Chris or Sabrina around, and I knew how to do it.

CHAPTER
TWENTY-FOUR

I exited through the lobby a few minutes later with my mind whirling.

My thoughts centered on a Malcolm Gladwell book I read about talking to strangers and what happens psychologically when we first meet someone. We have built-in lie detectors, but when we first meet someone, they are set to "off". We assume that everyone we meet for the first time is telling the truth during most everyday conversations. The only way this investigation made sense was that someone, or more than one person, had to be lying.

But who?

Like my conversation with Chris. What if his offer of helping me expand was a carrot? A plump, orange carrot dangled in front of me to shift my focus. Natasha said not to trust him or Sabrina. But everything about him seemed sincere. Maybe I'm lulled in because of his Scottish brogue. I don't know. Maybe I can't read him well because of the accent. I'd be thrilled if the guy narrated my life, to be honest. He had that kind of voice.

How could I verify if Sabrina and Chris were skimming tax money from the guests? They already told me that Natasha was wrong and gave me an explanation why. From their perspective, Natasha didn't need to know how they were handling refunds to the guests who were overcharged on the hospitality taxes. No one had questioned their bills, either during check-in or check-out or after the fact. It was a small amount, but small amounts added up.

Natasha lied to me. I knew that now. But did she lie about everything she told me, or was there a kernel of truth to her story? How could I prove it? There was one way. It was risky, but it might draw this entire thing to a close.

I sent her a text hoping that maybe, just maybe, she'd see it and get back to me.

As I walked up the street to the bookstore where I parked the Jeep, I looked back and saw Chris exiting through the side entrance of OceanScapes. He looked about but didn't see me. The night was black. Thick cloud cover overhead meant that the only illumination came from streetlights. The OceanScapes parking lot was well-lit, but I was on the sidewalk and up the street. I could see him, but because I wasn't near any streetlights, I was in shadow. Like a ninja. A pudgy, clumsy ninja.

I stood motionless while he strutted across the parking lot to his Harley parked out front. He straddled the hog, fired it up with a roar, and blasted off. He didn't know I was here. Could the desk clerk have heard Chris leaving? Would he have known that was Chris?

With the proliferation of motorcycles in Myrtle Beach, I wouldn't know how he could tell. Chris' bike was parked at an angle that couldn't be seen from the lobby. His exit through the side might mean that the desk clerk didn't know he was gone.

I sat on a nearby bench and watched the sparse traffic

coasting by. A plan formed in my head. I'd never done anything like it, few people have, but my curiosity was getting the best of me.

I needed to check on a few things first. I called the reporter, Erica.

"Hey, Clark. I was just thinking about you," she said upon answering.

The thought of a beautiful, voluptuous young woman thinking about me at any time sent a shiver down my spine.

"Oh, how so?" I said.

"Wondering if you've found anything?"

That was disappointing. If that's why she was thinking about me, then she must have bupkis too. "I've learned bits and pieces of things. I don't know if they fit together or matter."

"You want to get together and see if any of our pieces fit? I'm off tomorrow morning and don't have much to do."

She wasn't going to make keeping pervy thoughts out of my head easy with her unintended double entendres.

"Look, it's getting late. How about coffee in the morning? I'll buy you breakfast."

"Sounds good to me. Let me know when and where."

"I'll text you." We hung up a minute later. With the phone still in my hand, I called Gomez.

She answered after half a ring. "Yes, Clark."

"Hey, a couple quick questions if you don't mind."

She expelled an annoyed breath. "Go ahead. You know the rule. I'll only tell you what I'm allowed."

"I know. I know, and I appreciate your time and candor. Have you learned anything about the threats from the oil company?"

She laughed. "Yes, we have."

"Then why are you laughing?"

"It was a thirteen-year-old boy from Tajikistan."

It took me a moment to think about how to respond. When I didn't, Gomez filled in the gaps. "There's this computer whiz in a small village in a valley at the base of the Fann Mountains near the capital of Dushanbe. He pulled an email list from the internet and decided he was going to send everyone on it random threats. He thought he was smooth and could cover his tracks, but we have a girl at SLED who's smoother and tracked him down."

"Wait. Where is Tajikistan? I've heard of it but know nothing about it."

"It separates Afghanistan and China. I'd never given it a second thought until I heard this. Apparently, he started sending the threats when he was ten, and kept doing them over the years."

"I thought you said that they had been increasing in recent months."

"Yeah, when their authorities brought him in for questioning, he said that he had been out of school and was bored."

"How did he get her info to begin with?"

"That's the interesting part, and something we're going to have to pass on to another agency. Apparently, he got her name off the dark web."

"The dark web?"

"Yeah, it's a collection of websites that operate outside of search engines. You need certain software, authorizations, and configurations to access them. It's a hotbed of criminal activity."

"Like going to the Red-Light District after two a.m.?"

"Worse. It turns out that one of the companies that wanted to drill off the Carolina coast put Paige's info out on the dark web after she started raising a fuss. This kid got it, and they started paying him to send her threats."

"Did they know he was ten?"

"Nope. They thought he was a thirty-something-year-old from Yonkers. He had them fooled."

"Which oil company was it?"

"I can't say, but they're one of the biggest. They have gas stations all over the country."

I digested the information and wondered if someone could get my personal data off the dark web. I swallowed before continuing. "So, Paige and her husband started getting these threats and assumed it was from the oil companies?"

"That sums it up. What else you got, Clark? Time is pressing."

"Find any witnesses who might have seen Paige being carried to the bookstore?"

Gomez sighed. "Nope. We can't find anyone who saw anything in the three blocks between OceanScapes and your bookstore. It's like the only time in Myrtle Beach's history that no one was around. I swear we're like New York, but we're the 'Beach That Never Sleeps.'"

My eyebrows arched. "That's the truth."

"Here's another. Does Martin the VP have an alibi?"

"Why him?"

"Because he got passed over to take over the company after Mr. John retires for Paige."

"Yeah, we knew about that. He was mad, but he's also near

retirement. In the end, he didn't want to take that on. Besides, he was dropping off his grandkids at daycare that morning in Carolina Forest. We have it on video. He couldn't have killed Paige."

"That settles that. What about the keycard log?"

"Nope. The last entrant was from the night before. The first swipe that morning came from the cleaning woman."

I couldn't come up with any further questions that would lead to brief answers, so I said, "Thank you, and I appreciate your time, Gomez."

"Listen, between you and me, the circumstances of this case have us flummoxed. We don't like regular citizens aiding in investigations because they get in our way and could get hurt or wind up in a body bag themselves. You haven't gotten in the way, just kind of operating on the fringes, and from what I gather, you don't seem to be close enough on any lead to have angered anyone." My brain flitted to Chris' bulging biceps. "From here on in, it might be best if you leave this to us."

I knew that would not happen. "Well, I don't want to get hurt, or have something worse happen to me."

"That's not a promise, Clark."

I sighed. "Okay, okay. I'll back off."

"Good. You already lost your wife. It'd be a shame if something happened to you, too."

Odd. Was that a threat?

CHAPTER
TWENTY-FIVE

Upon reentering, I strolled past the desk. The clerk was typing something into his phone, leaning back against a credenza, looking bored. I couldn't blame him. At this time of the evening during mid-week, the bookstore was usually dead. The same probably went for the OceanScapes lobby several hours after check-in time. His name tag identified him as Kevin.

"Hey, Kevin," I said, catching his attention.

He looked up like he was surprised to see anyone in the lobby this late. Recognition struck. "Oh, yes, sir. Good to see you again."

I held up my phone. "Chris called and told me I left something in his office. Told me he'd meet me at the elevators with it."

"Oh, cool," he said. He led me back to the door leading to the restricted area, slid his card through the reader, and popped it open. "Go ahead."

"Thanks, man."

"No problem, sir," he said and returned to his previous position.

I ducked through the employee entryway into the back hall. No one was around. Besides the hum of air moving through the ducts in the ceiling, all was quiet. The lights were dimmer than when I was here earlier. They must lower the level in the off hours to conserve electricity.

Upon reaching the elevator bank, I reached a sweaty hand into my back pocket and withdrew Natasha's keycard. Moment of truth. Here we go.

I turned nonchalantly to see if the desk clerk had poked his head through the entryway or if someone had entered the hall during the time it took me to walk from the lobby to here. Nope. Not a peep.

I took a deep breath and slid her keycard through the reader on the wall. The little LED light turned from red to green. I breathed out.

No alarms. No one rushed to stop me. I returned the keycard to my back pocket while hoping no one would be in the elevator when it opened.

I swallowed. The door slid open. I stood off to one side in case someone needed to step off. If someone did, I would say I was looking for the bathroom. Unless they recognized me. In that case, I had no plan.

The elevator car was empty. I stepped in believing that whatever happened after the car opened on the second floor would change my life.

Little did I realize how much it would.

* * *

I looked both ways before exiting the elevator. No one was coming or going. One light shone on the entire floor from above the elevators. Its effect diminished outside of fifteen feet, leaving the rest of the office level in darkness. I did not see any office lights emanating through the cracks in any office door in either direction. I was alone.

I had perhaps ten minutes to sneak around up here before the desk clerk might become suspicious. If he did at all. Better to be safe than sorry.

The camera on the wall across from the elevators still had black paint on it. It was a relief that no one had exchanged the camera for a new one in the fifteen minutes I was gone.

I crept down the hall as quiet as I could. Every footstep in the flip-flops seemed to echo off the walls. I never noticed the loud snap of the sole on my heel every time I raised my foot before now. Perhaps I was being overly aware of any noises I made right now. A heightened sense of awareness. Or was it guilt from trespassing?

Upon reaching Sabrina's door, I gave it a light rap. The hollow knock of my knuckles on wood seemed to reverberate throughout the hall. In truth, the sound couldn't be heard over five feet away, but my conscience amplified the noise.

No answer came.

I slid the keycard through the reader on the door. The light went from red to green. The latch gave way. The door opened. I fumbled for the light switch. As my hand brushed against it, I realized that wasn't a good idea. I closed the door and pulled out my phone, turning on the flashlight function.

Blood whooshed through my ears, caused by my thudding heart. I took small, shallow breaths to calm myself. Closing my eyes, I pictured me sitting on a beach with Autumn at a lower latitude with a beer in my hand, watching waves roll in across a blue-watered bay. I smiled.

My eyes reopened. At this point, I couldn't control what would happen if they caught me here. It was out of my hands. I had to focus. The mental stopwatch I had going told me I had five minutes.

A narrow beam of light protruded from next to the camera lens on the back of the phone. People pay hundreds of dollars for these phones that are pocket computers, but one overlooked — and in this case lifesaving — feature was the flashlight. Like Chris' office, the only window in Sabrina's office was up high behind her desk. Hopefully, no one from the street behind OceanScapes would see the beam of light from my phone moving through the darkness through the window.

Her office was arranged like Chris'. A seating group to my left upon entering sat atop the now familiar style of rug. Beyond that was a desk and a wall of shelving. A row of filing cabinets lined the left side of the room. She had twice as many as Chris.

I padded across the floor in a crouch, stopping in front of the third cabinet. Natasha said I would find what I needed in the third drawer about halfway back. There would be two folders. One for people who had tax money refunded, and one for those who hadn't.

I froze. Uh oh. There was a lock at the top of each cabinet. The lock accepted only round keys. I thumbed the latch on the top drawer. It slid out. I got on my tiptoes and flicked through the drawer, noting the file names. Everything was neat and orderly. The same went for the other drawers.

When I got to the third drawer down, the one Natasha told me about, it didn't open. Locked.

Cursing to myself, I was unsure of what to do. Natasha said nothing about the cabinets being locked. It makes sense, though.

Sabrina handled a lot of money and transactions records. She had access to guests' credit card information. Of course, she would lock that down.

But Natasha swore the evidence was there. I looked over at Sabrina's desk. It was tidy. Everything had a place. Every place had a thing. She wouldn't leave incriminating documents out in the open.

There was nothing more I could do here. I'm not a lock picker. A nose picker on occasion, yes, but not one to pick locks.

I had one more play up here. The timer in my head ran low.

I doused the light and cracked open the door. No one stirred in either direction. I snuck out, closed the door behind me, and sneaked over to Chris' office.

The keycard worked there as well.

But as the LED turned from red to green on the card reader, the elevator sounded. Ping. My heart leaped into my throat.

The clunk of plastic wheels hitting tile reached my ears as I whipped open the door and closed it. Panic tried to settle in. Did Chris come back? Was it the desk clerk?

I did the only thing I could think of. I ran across the office, squeezed myself into a ball and hid under Chris' desk. The lights in the hall came on. A broad beam of light streamed across the floor emanating from the bottom of the door.

If Chris came in, I was screwed. He would pick me up and toss me out the second-story window. Probably.

I crammed myself in the kickspace between the modesty panel at the front of the desk, his rolling chair, and the trash can. Five minutes passed. Then ten. The mental timer I started when I stepped into the elevator downstairs went off a long time ago. That was gone.

This was such a wasted gamble. Natasha got me. Hook, line, and sinker. She had me believing Chris and Sabrina were behind Paige's death. I did the stupid thing and accepted everything the beautiful woman told me as gospel.

When I read that Malcolm Gladwell book about talking to strangers and the examples he gave of people being fooled upon first meeting someone, I thought that could never be me. I'm a people. I thought I knew when people were lying to me.

It turns out, I was the fool.

I was figuring out what I would say to the desk clerk in the lobby if I made it back downstairs when the door opened.

It startled me so much that I jerked and hit my head on the bottom of the desk.

Whoever was at the door shrieked. She was as scared of me as I was of her.

"Who's in here?" came an accented voice.

Busted.

The lights flicked on. I had no choice. Raising my hands, I unfolded myself out from under the desk. My knees, neck, and about every other joint in my body cracked and protested.

"Don't be alarmed," I called as I turned around and see who was at the door. That's when I looked down.

And everything changed.

CHAPTER
TWENTY-SIX

Several hours later, after having handcuffs put on me, me pleading for the cops to call Detective Gomez, pleading with Gomez, a call to Mr. John, a call to all the dramatis personae, and having the handcuffs taken off, all gathered in Sabrina's office. Even Natasha reappeared from her hiding place for this. Two uniformed officers stood in the doorway.

This was taking an enormous gamble on meeting here rather than Chris' office first.

The owner, John Sullivan, sat in Sabrina's chair. Chris stood at his left shoulder and Martin to his right. Natasha and Sabrina sat in the two guest chairs turned to face Gomez, Moody and me. Linda held a cup of steaming coffee in one hand, leaning against a wall next to Tanzee. Like sardines in a can. Officers O'Brien and Nichols stood against the door.

"Okay, Clark," Gomez said. "We're all here. What's this about?"

Here it was. The moment of truth. Here goes. "I thought I would tell you all who killed Paige."

Gomez placed a hand on my wrist. "Are you sure we shouldn't discuss this first?"

This was a scene I had envisioned myself doing. I've seen it done dozens of times in movies, TV, and books. The Summation. Where the investigator called all the key players together and unraveled how the poor victim met their fate and who committed the heinous crime. This was my moment.

"No, no," I assured her. "I have it figured out."

She regarded me with discerning eyes. "Okay."

The others awaited.

John Sullivan's carefully coifed hair—even at three o'clock in the morning—shifted to the side. "Please, Mr. Thomas. I want to know so we can begin to put this tragedy behind us."

"Thank you, Mr. Sullivan. Here's how it went down." Clearing my throat, I said, "Paige arrived here early yesterday morning to complete the payroll before a family vacation. She knew that she could slip in, do her work, and slip out the side relatively unseen. She sneaked in through the side entrance at 6:57. The cameras caught that. Gomez, when did the cameras go black?"

"At 7:11."

"So, fourteen minutes after Paige arrived, someone spray painted the cameras. Enough time for them to lie in wait and see if she was going to come back out before doing the deed. Mr. John?"

"Yes, son?"

"Who has access to that side entrance?"

"Those of us who work on the upper floor."

"That narrows it down, doesn't it?"

"It does," Gomez concurred.

"Did the camera show anyone approaching it before it went black?"

"Nope. Whoever did it knew the sight lines of the camera

and how to sneak up on it." She cast a judgmental eye at Mr. John. "Not the best of setups."

"Again, sounds like an inside job, doesn't it?" I said.

Mr. John, Natasha, Martin, and Linda nodded their heads in agreement. Moody grunted.

"Before we get to how, let's talk about why, shall we? Motive."

"Yes, let's get to it," Mr. John demanded.

"Yes, sir. Natasha came to me yesterday after Paige's death and told me she suspected Sabrina and Chris of tax fraud. Why come to me and not Gomez first?"

"Yes, Natasha," Gomez said, "why wouldn't you tell us when we questioned you yesterday? You know, you running off makes it look like you have something to hide."

Natasha held out a plaintive hand. "Look, look. It is a habit from my old country. We don't trust the police. They are crooked? My fellow villagers knew that the polizei caused as many problems as they solved. I know Clark from shopping at his store and he seemed to be a smart guy. Maybe a snoop. I took a chance and asked for his help."

Chris stirred and shifted his feet. "Come on. It's late. I have to catch an early flight tomorrow."

"Have some patience, Mr. McInally," Gomez said. "I'm sure Clark will wrap this all up soon. Right, Clark?"

"I am. We have another stop to make. But this shouldn't take long."

"Thank you, Mr. Thomas," Mr. John said. "Proceed."

"Thanks," I said. "Now, where was I? Oh, right. Tax fraud, or skimming, or whatever you want to call it. Theft is another word I'd use. I asked Sabrina about this and I must thank her for indulging me and my curiosity."

Mr. John leaned forward and looked between Chris and Sabrina. He demanded, "What is this about?"

Sabrina, to her credit, explained. "Do you remember when the city stopped sending the extra percentage of the hospitality tax to Horry County?" He nodded along with the rest of the room. It was a big topic last year. Sabrina continued, "Well, when we had to change our system, it was only charging the adjusted rate to new guests. Ones who had never been here before. But it charged the old, higher rate, to returning guests. I caught on to that and started sending refund checks with apology letters to the ones affected. I explained all of this to Clark this morning, and I don't know why we're here. I have a paper trail proving it."

"As is proper," Mr. John said. "What of it? Where's the theft?"

Time to put a coin in the slot machine, pull the lever and see what happens. Hopefully a row of cherries.

I raised a finger at Sabrina. "You say you have a folder on this?"

"I do."

"So, when a returning guest comes in, and slides their card through the reader, they get the old tax percentage?"

"Correct. At the end of the day, I batch out the cards and go through them to see if I need make any refunds. The guy who does our point-of-sale system is working on it. I told you all of this."

"You did. You did. And I appreciate it." I was losing the room. Tanzee examined her nails. Time to get to the point and pull the handle on my imaginary slot machine. "What about those who pay with cash?"

That stopped her. She glanced at Chris, but he kept his eyes forward, staring at something in the far corner of the room or outer space. Anywhere but here.

The execs and Mr. John murmured. The vibe in the room changed. Now to prove it, thanks to Natasha.

I said to Gomez, "If you'll go over to the third file cabinet on the wall there, and open the third drawer down, you'll find a file for guest refunds. The one Sabrina was talking about doing the right thing with. But if you move towards the back, you will find another folder. One with cash receipts that aren't refunded."

Her eyes bored into mine. I couldn't tell if she thought I was insane or if she was weighing whether to trust me. Her chin bobbed up and down. "Okay, Clark. Let's see what we have here."

She went to the cabinet, reached down, and thumbed the release. The drawer held. "Sabrina, do you have a key?"

Sabrina's eyes bulged. She looked to Chris, hoping he would answer. He stared at her, perhaps hoping the same. Their reaction was all that I hoped for. It was a damning moment, and they knew it. Now we all did. It was her office. Any display of reticence would indicate guilt.

After one last disapproving glance at Chris, she pulled a keyring out of her pocket, jangled through the keys, picked one, and held it up to Gomez.

A minute later, the incriminating file sat on the desk before Mr. John. His face turned red. "I am so disappointed in you, Sabrina. I thought you were better than this."

"I'm so sorry, Mr. John." Sabrina cried. "I didn't think it was that big of a deal. It was a couple dollars here and there. I didn't think it was worth the trouble to refund the money."

"How much did it add up to?" Gomez said.

Sabrina rubbed a hand across her chin. "I don't know. A couple thousand, I think."

"Grand larceny," Gomez said and turned to me. "Okay, so what's your theory? Sabrina killed Paige?"

"On Monday evening," I said, ignoring the question for now, "Natasha met with Paige where she told her of her suspicions about Sabrina. It got heated. I have a witness. He said he heard Paige and someone else arguing through the office walls while he was waiting to clock out."

Sabrina opened her mouth, but no words came out. I spoke for her.

"The witness's name is Solomon. Young kid. Loves his Incredible Hulk. Anyway, Natasha stormed out of the meeting. Chris told me that after Natasha left Paige's office, she called Sabrina in. I don't know the conclusion of that meeting, but I suspect Paige was going to tell the executive staff yesterday before her trip. Sabrina knew that and had one chance to stop her, but she needed help."

"Listen, I didn't do it," Sabrina said, "You have no proof of it, anyway."

I held up a finger. "I never said you did. Which leads us to our second stop."

"Where's that?" Gomez said.

"Follow me."

I led everyone from the room. Most groaned in protest as they got to their feet. Time to end this.

I led everyone from the office and down the hall. This was a quick trip.

Gomez stepped up beside me. "You know we can't all go into Paige's office, don't you?"

"There's no need. We're stopping before that." I stopped in front of Chris' door. "Here we are."

Chris stormed to the front of the group and stood toe to toe with me. "What do you mean, 'Here we are?' What's the meaning of this?"

O'Brien stepped between us and put a hand on Chris' chest. "Back away, please."

Chris backed off two steps. To me, he said, "Well?"

"Proof," I answered.

"Proof? There is no proof. I didn't do anything."

"If that's the case," Gomez said, "Then you won't mind opening this door."

Chris narrowed his eyes at her and then me. "You know what? I'll open the door. I'm curious what Clark here is going to try to pin on me."

He slid his card through the reader and opened the door.

"Thank you," Gomez said. "Please step aside. Clark? After you."

I flipped on the light. Everyone filed in behind me and I waited until the officers had taken up station by the door.

"Okay, Clark," Mr. John said. "We're all here. Get on with it."

"Yes, sir," I said. "Thank you. By Monday evening, Sabrina knew she was in trouble and possibly going to jail. Not wanting that to happen, she enlisted help in the form of her boyfriend, Chris."

"Not true!" Sabrina and Chris shouted.

"See," I said, undaunted, "they're on the same page. Sabrina needed Paige and Natasha gone. She knew that Natasha lived with several roommates, and that getting her alone by herself would present a challenge. So, she went after the low-hanging fruit first. Paige. She was close with Paige and was aware of her schedule. Specifically, that Paige did the payroll early on Tuesday mornings.

"On Monday night, she and Chris devised a plan to murder her. They waited near the parking lot, out of visual range for Paige to see. They could see her, but she couldn't see them. After Paige let herself in, they counted ten minutes before Chris blacked out the cameras. They went into her office, confronted her, and whacked her over the head with something before rolling her in the rug and carrying her up Flagg Street."

"That's a lie," Chris said. "I wasn't anywhere near here."

I crossed my arms. "Then why is the murder weapon behind your desk?"

That stopped him. And everyone else in the room.

To his credit, Chris recovered quickly. "Excuse me?"

"You're excused," I said, "but not from murdering Paige. How long have you worked here?"

"Uh, two years."

"Then why do you have a service award for a seven-year anniversary? Gomez, would you mind stepping over here and reading what's written on the inscription of this specific trophy?"

I pointed to an award on his trophy wall. It was a flat square, about six inches to each side, consisting of four pewter interlocking puzzle pieces, and sat atop a walnut stand. A silver engraved plate with black lettering faced the wood.

"Sure thing." She stepped past me, leaned in for a closer

look at the trophy, cleared her throat, and said, "Awarded for excellent teamwork on your seventh work anniversary. Paige Whitaker."

The officers at the door stood straight. Everyone, except Sabrina, backed away a step, or as much as possible in the confined space of the office, from Chris.

"Would you care to explain this?" Gomez said to Chris.

His mouth opened a few times, but no words came out. Like Sabrina, I filled them in for him.

"When you confronted Paige," I said, "you grabbed the first thing you saw and struck her with it, then ditched this in your office, hoping no one would see it for a few days before you could dispose of it."

"That's not true," Chris protested. "I don't know how that got there! I'm innocent, I tell you! Someone planted that."

"Sure, sure," I said. "Gomez, do you have a glove on you?"

"Of course," she said, reaching into her pocket and pulling one out.

"Would you mind putting it on, reach under his desk, and pull out the top item in the trash can?"

Her brows joined like a caterpillar, but she pulled on the glove and ducked down. She rummaged around in the trash can out of everyone's view and stood a moment later.

She held up a black spray paint can.

Another, louder gasp came from the room.

Chris' mouth dropped open and his eyes went wide.

I had dropped the hammer on him.

It was his turn to hit back.

CHAPTER
TWENTY-SEVEN

He stared at me a moment before bursting out laughing. Sabrina, Mr. John, and the other executives joined him.

Gomez put a hand on my arm. "Clark, that can't be."

A lump formed in my throat as my heart threatened to burst out of my chest. I laid it down for them with certainty that I was right. Chris did it. I proved it. Except...

"Clark, my friend, I should be insulted that you would think I would kill poor Paige, but I loved her like a sister. She took me in when I moved here and made me feel at home. I stayed at her house for weeks after starting work here, bunking in one of her kid's rooms. We became close, both with her and her husband. I would never harm Paige."

"How do you explain the award and spray paint?" Let's see him try to smooth talk his way out of those pieces of evidence.

"I don't know, my friend. Someone was trying to set me up. I mean, my office is next door to Paige's. It would be the closest place to ditch the murder weapon and spray paint. Besides—"

"Besides what?" I said.

"Clark, Clark, Clark," Mr. John said. "Chris was thirty-five thousand feet in the air at the time Paige was killed."

The bomb went off in my chest. I didn't know what a heart

attack felt like, but I imagined that the pain in my sternum was that but dialed back a notch. Still painful. "Wait, what?"

"If you had run this by me and Moody before you tried this, Clark," Gomez said with a cross between a scolding and consoling tone in her voice, "I would have told you that Chris had an alibi. It checked out. Sabrina picked him up over at the airport after he landed around eleven yesterday morning."

The pain in my chest subsided, but now my cheeks were on fire.

Chris' expression aimed at me wasn't one of anger. Thank goodness. I still didn't want to meet him in their dark basement garage, though.

"Listen mate," he said. "I understand you wanted to help find Paige's killer. Believe me, we all do. I won't hold this against you. I was serious when I said I wanted to help you and your business, and I still do. You got caught up in the moment."

"I appreciate that," I said.

Chris stepped away from Sabrina. "I know you've been getting a lot of new cars lately. I thought you said the money was coming from your dad?"

Sabrina wiped her nose across the back of her wrist. "That wasn't entirely true."

"We'll talk about all of this later," he said.

She sobbed. "Okay."

I said to Gomez, "What now?"

"That's up to Mr. John," she said. "He's the one who has to decide if he's going to press charges for breaking and entering and what to do with Sabrina."

At least that part of my summation was correct. I busted them. At least, Sabrina was busted.

Gomez looked at Mr. John. "What do you think?"

My life hung on his next few words. I pictured myself making tick marks on a gray concrete wall behind bars, counting the days away in prison.

He rubbed his chin. "We can let Clark go."

The breath I expelled was loud enough to wake the guests in their rooms across the street.

"Thank you, Mr. John," I said. "Thank you. Thank you. Thank you."

He held up a hand. "Save it. The only reason I'm not pressing charges is because of what you found showing that Sabrina was shortchanging guests. Even if it was only a few pennies. Refund the money. No matter how much trouble it is to do it. I don't care if we lose money on the cost of postage, the envelopes, the checks written, and the time in payroll it takes for you to do it." He slammed a fist on Chris' desk. "It's the right thing to do, Sabrina."

Sabrina jumped — we all did — and held a hand to the top of her chest. "I'm so sorry, Mr. John. I didn't think it was worth the time. No one ever knew or asked."

"'Sorry' doesn't cut it, Sabrina. You're fired. I don't care if that means we don't have anyone trained for HR at present. We'll figure it out. We always have."

Gomez guided me from the office while the people from OceanScapes discussed the night's events. I feared for Natasha's job. Linda escorted us to the elevator and used her keycard to give us access.

Once we exited the building, Gomez thanked the officers and sent them on their way.

She, Moody, and I stood outside the doors and watched

them climb into their patrol car and speed away into the Myrtle Beach night. Waves crashed across the street. A cicada trilled nearby. No traffic passed on Ocean Boulevard.

It was Gomez, Moody, and I.

"Look, Clark," she said, "I appreciate you wanting to help us out, but there's a reason we're professionals. All the book reading and movie watching in the world can't train or prepare you for our jobs. I know there's an entire market for books with stories about amateur sleuths, but that doesn't happen in real life."

"I know. I just wanted to help."

She placed a hand on my shoulder. "I know you did. You did something few people ever do, much less volunteer to do. That says something about you, Clark. You got moxie. I'll give you that."

My lips formed a tight smile. "Thank you. What now?"

"Go home. Get some rest. Carry on with your life. Try to forget about all of this. That's an order."

"Yes, ma'am."

"If you think of anything that could help, don't hesitate."

"I'll do that."

Moody grunted and gave me a sympathetic pat on the arm. It helped.

We parted. They climbed into their unmarked car. I hiked back to my Jeep with my head hung low.

I went home, turned off my phone, drank half a bottle of rum, and passed out on top of the made bed in my bedroom until that afternoon.

CHAPTER
TWENTY-EIGHT

———————————

Gomez told me to forget about all of this. I disobeyed her as soon as I awoke.

The answer was obvious as to how I got it wrong. I didn't check alibis. Rookie mistake. I had motive and means. Chris was big and strong enough to strike the killing blow and carry Paige over his shoulder for a few blocks.

Looking back on it, I put forth a flimsy motive. Sure, Sabrina had reason to cover her tracks with the hospitality tax theft. Had I thought about it from her perspective, I would have realized that, okay, so Natasha figured it out. If I were going to kill Paige to cover it up, Natasha would have to be next. Right?

In that case, what if Natasha told her roommates? How many of them were there to whack to cover her tracks? What about the other people at the desk? They have access to the same receipts Natasha did. She said she figured it out first. How can I be sure of that if I'm Sabrina? Might as well club them over the head and pile up the bodies.

Not only did my theory with Sabrina now seem implausible, her roping Chris into it made me understand why all of the executives laughed at me. Chris had a close bond with Paige. Sabrina and Paige were good buddies as well. And Chris was on a flight.

By my count, that's three strikes. I'm out.

Did I want to be, though? I wanted to pick up the bat and step into the batter's box again.

After clearing the gunk out of my eyes, I reached over and held the power button on the side of my phone to turn it on. I let it go through the startup process while I rolled over onto my back.

Our bedroom had two windows. Yes, I still call it "ours." Autumn loved her sleep almost above anything. She bought some of those expensive, top-of-the-line blackout curtains. It didn't surprise me that I slept all day. The room was dark enough to make a coal miner uncomfortable. Made it great for sleeping during the daytime.

I sat on the edge of the bed, checking for missed calls and messages.

There weren't many. Surprising. One voicemail from Karen to see where I was. If I didn't show up at the store, her and Margaret could handle things without me. There were no messages or calls from Gomez, Natasha, or from anyone at OceanScapes. I wasn't sure whether to feel relieved or disappointed.

Mom had sent me a text in the middle of the afternoon, inviting me over for dinner. She said there was a pot roast in the slow cooker. The clock on the phone read 5:23. I could make that.

* * *

Later, I was buttering a soft yeast roll at my parents' dinner table. A platter of sliced beef, potatoes, and carrots sat in the center. A pot of steaming Velveeta shells — a family staple — sat to one side. Add in a pitcher of sweet tea and an apple pie baking in the oven, and you had a classic Thomas family dinner.

Dad had a college basketball game between Southern Methodist and UL-Lafayette playing on the TV in the corner with the sound turned off. What interest he could have in that game was beyond me. To each his own, I guess.

Mom asked, "How was your day, Clark?"

It was going to come up anyway. Might as well get it out of the way.

"I just woke up."

"Take a nap today?"

"Nope." I sliced into the pot roast. My fork cut through like a hot knife through butter. I took a bite and chewed, letting her question hang in the air while I savored the meat. Mom waited. Dad's eyes were glued to the game. "I was out late last night and didn't get home until near sunrise."

"You weren't out partying, were you? On a Wednesday?"

I wanted to get defensive and tell her that didn't concern her. If I wanted to stay out late, I could. That was something I never did, though. I liked being in bed by ten with a book in my hand every night. She knew that. But you can't tell your parents not to worry about you no matter how old you are.

"No, no. I was at OceanScapes."

"What were you doing there?"

"Trying to wrap up the case," I said, as though I was officially part of the investigation.

"I take it you didn't," she said.

I stuffed a potato in my mouth. "Nope. Not even close."

"What happened?"

I told her how I gathered everyone together and did my best television detective impersonation with the summation and how I blew it by not checking alibis first.

She chewed on that for a minute without responding. Dad had even turned his attention from the game to my narration.

"Wait," he said. "You took this keycard this girl gave you and snuck around the offices of that place trying to find evidence of a crime that didn't concern you?"

"I did."

"I'm going to tell you point blank, son. That was stupid."

Mom glared at him. "Lloyd! Be nice. That must have been hard on him."

Leave it to Mom to have my back. But Dad wasn't finished.

"Clark, do you know how stupid and careless you were in doing that? You could have gone to jail. You could have lost your business. You could still lose your standing in the business community."

If Mr. John carries through with what he said he was going to do, I probably would. I didn't know what to say.

Dad did. "Son, what on earth were you thinking?"

"Like I said, I had a feeling that I needed to do something. That's the truth."

"Listen, I know you're still healing from the loss of Autumn. But you can't go around trying to solve murders to make up for it."

"Why not?"

He ticked off the points on his fingers. "Well, you're not a cop, for one. You're not trained. It could be dangerous. A suspect could kill you to hide their crime. You get the point?"

"Look, everything you said is true. Everything you said I took into consideration... after diving headlong into trying to solve the murder. I promised this girl, Natasha, that I would help her. I couldn't stop."

"Yes, you could have."

"How?"

"By going about your normal life and letting the police handle it. Like a normal person would have. Take yourself out of it. What would change if you hadn't gotten involved? Did you find anything the police didn't know or wouldn't eventually learn?"

That brought me up short. I chewed on another potato. Gomez and Moody would have spoken with Solomon. He would have told him about the confrontation he witnessed the night before Paige's death. That would have led to Natasha for a second round of questioning. Then Gomez would learn about Natasha's suspicions of the tax theft.

What else was there?

"Nothing, I guess," I said.

"See," Dad said, and cut into his pot roast and turned his attention back to the ball game. He had made is point.

Mom took a sip of tea. "Tell me how you arrived at your conclusion that it had to have been Chris."

I laid it out, trying not to omit any details.

At the end, she said, "You erred in not checking motive, but you already know that. Like your dad said, you have no training. You fit a few clues together and jumped to the conclusion that it had to have been Chris. Well, it's not. Are you going to keep after this?"

"Gomez told me to back off."

"That didn't answer my question, Clark."

I rubbed a hand over my face and punctured a stray carrot with my fork. "I don't know. I feel like I lost. Game over. I screwed it all up, and I doubt that anyone will give me the time of day now."

"Son, life isn't a game. People's lives aren't a game. There's nothing more fragile and valuable than life. If someone kills another person, then justice should be served."

"Nancy don't encourage him," Dad said.

She ignored him. "What else do you have?"

"To be honest, I had keyed in on Chris so much that I tried to develop a storyline based on him, Sabrina, and the tax theft."

"Well, forget about that. What could be missing? What other motives might there be?"

"There were two. The oil companies might want revenge, and there might have been some friction with other executives. They named Paige to take over the company instead of the VP. He was upset about it but has an alibi."

"What about the oil companies?"

I shrugged and took a bite of a roll. "Some kid in Tajikistan with too much time on his hands was sending threats to random emails he got off the dark web."

"I don't understand a word you just said."

"I'm not sure I understand either. It was this brainiac kid with nothing better to do."

"That's wild."

"That's the world today. Gotta be careful online."

She took a sip of tea and set the glass back down on the table. "Here's my pair of pennies. Start from scratch. Get to the nuts and bolts. You all haven't found a motive or suspect yet.

Something else happened that you don't know about. Push all of that aside. Look at the crime itself. Perhaps the answer is there. Tell me what happened as though you were telling it to me for the first time."

I shoved a piece of pot roast in my mouth and washed it down with tea while I composed my thoughts.

"Okay, Paige went to OceanScapes on Tuesday morning just before seven to work on payroll before her vacation. At eleven minutes after seven, the first camera was spray-painted over. The second one happened a minute later."

"How did they do that without being seen?"

"Whoever did it somehow knew the sight lines of the cameras and how to sneak around under them, out of view."

"It had to be an inside job."

"Yes. The killer clubbed her over the head and rolled her up in the rug. He went over to Chris' office and planted the evidence. Returned, got Paige, carried her down the steps and up the street before tossing her at my back door without being seen."

"How do you know they weren't seen?"

"There's no cameras on that part of Flagg Street. They haven't found any eyewitnesses."

"What caused him to dump her at your place?"

"I'm not sure. The alcove at the bookstore would have been the first one they came to. The woman who owns the t-shirt shop a couple doors down had her back door open, throwing out boxes. Could be that the killer saw her, got spooked, and dumped the body before she saw them."

"Hmm. Okay, let's back up to the crime scene. Was there any evidence in Paige's office?"

I explained the layout of the office first. "They said someone had moved the furniture in the seating group to the side so they could get the rug out to roll Paige in."

"What kind of flooring is underneath the rug?"

"Carpet."

"What kind of carpet?"

"Regular carpet, I guess. Tan."

"That could have muffled any sound."

"Perhaps. The area that's underneath the offices are where their break room and other work areas are. There was one guy working the desk that morning, and he said he didn't hear anything. The timecards were scattered all over the area near her desk and her chair was overturned. That's all there was."

She stuck a potato in her mouth and chewed on it and the scenario while Dad popped open a PBR, sat back in his dining room chair, and watched the game. He hoovered his food, leaving a spotless plate behind. As he always did. It was a habit he had picked up while he was in the Marines in Vietnam. Eat quick, you never knew when you had to rush into action. I dashed some parmesan cheese on my macaroni before having a bite.

"It's baffling," Mom said. "You have no witnesses. No camera feeds. No one heard anything. No one saw anything. They left no evidence behind." She pointed her fork in my direction. "Think outside the box. Conventional means won't solve this. Leave it to the pros."

We were quiet a minute while we ate. Dad got up during a commercial break to get the pie out of the oven.

"I've read dozens, hundreds, of mystery novels throughout my life," I said. "Nora Roberts, Arthur Conan Doyle, John

Sandford, Dorothy Sayers, Sue Grafton, and the like. I always wondered how I would handle a murder investigation. Now that I'm living it, I've tried to think of what I could be missing. What did they do? How did they piece together their crimes?"

"You tell me. You seem to have compiled a lot of information about Paige. What are your instincts telling you? I know you have good instincts, Clark. I've seen them in action — in the business world, not this."

I leaned my head back, closed my eyes and put a hand over them. "You know what comes to mind? A book by John Lescroart called The Motive. Lescroart is a master of writing a compelling mystery. Might be the first book I remember reading that lays out what detectives are looking for. Means, motive, and opportunity. We discussed this the other day, but now for some reason, that book popped into my head."

"Okay. Let's put it together. Who had the means to do this?"

I held up a finger. "Here's the thing with that. We don't know who was there or who it could be. They can track keycard swipes when people enter the office areas. No one could have gotten up to Paige's office without one and it would have shown up on the report."

"Alright. We'll put the means part aside for a minute. Motive. Who had that?"

"There's Chris and Sabrina. Paige knew what they were up to, thanks to Natasha. But they have an ironclad alibi. They're out. Martin, the VP, got passed over to take over the company after the owner retires for Paige."

"Could he have done it?"

"Nope. They have him on camera dropping off his grandkids at a daycare in Carolina Forest."

"Who else?"

"The people from the offshore drilling corporation. They had it out for Paige after all of her activities to raise awareness for what they wanted to do."

"Yes, that was a horrible idea. The drilling. Some greedy, greedy people involved, but it happened two years ago."

"Yeah, that's what I'm thinking. I mean, I think I've spoken to everyone on the periphery of this thing already."

"I hate to keep egging you on, but you can always go back and talk to them if you think of anything else. Or reach out to that detective."

"But I don't know who at OceanScapes would talk to me at this point. The impression that I had was that they thought it was kind of sweet that I was looking into it. Like it was an honorable thing to do. After last night, no one will take me seriously. I blew it."

She shrugged. "Well, try to forget about it then."

And I did that.

Until Monday morning.

CHAPTER
TWENTY-NINE

Life returned to a sense of normalcy throughout the course of the week and weekend. I emailed the publisher of the ghostwriting work-in-progress that I would be a few days late completing the work.

The OceanScapes employees stopped coming to the store. Their bosses may have warned them to stay away. I would have if I were them. With my tail stuck between my legs, I did not attempt to contact anyone there either.

My botched summation and accusation against Chris seemed like it had been kept quiet. None of the regular local customers mentioned it.

Paige's murder investigation went silent.

The news stopped reporting on it after a few days as another story shoved it aside. A fire broke out in one of the high rises off 27th Avenue South that took the headlines. A guest called 911 after hearing the smoke alarm going off in a nearby room on the 19th floor. While he was waiting for the fire department to come, he grabbed a fire extinguisher from the hallway, broke through the door, and put out the flames.

The room was unoccupied with minimal damage. The fifteen hotel guests that night had to be evacuated. The mayor deemed the man who called in the fire as a hero and awarded him a commendation.

It turned out that the manager of the family-owned hotel lit the fire to collect insurance money.

I wondered if they called Gomez in to help investigate.

The weekend passed. Monday came. It was a typical Monday. The day started like many other Mondays. With a problem.

The credit card reader would not accept payments. I spent the first hour after opening the store on hold with the company who sold us the reader and cash register. We could only accept cash during that first hour and had to turn away some business. Rather than letting the coffee I brewed prior to opening go stale, we gave everyone a free cup, including the cash-paying customers.

After that was resolved, I told Margaret I was taking a break and left the store. I decided to check in with Marilyn at the comic shop. The last time I heard from her was at the Downtown Development Corporation meeting last week.

I wore a light jacket as my feet hit the sidewalk. A thick bank of clouds made its way from inland out over the ocean. The sun shone on the water in the distance beyond the clouds. Grayness shrouded my trip up to the Boardwalk proper. The local meteorologist forecasted scattered rain for the afternoon. Their forecasts are hit and miss with predicting precipitation. The ocean plays tricks with their models.

Looking at the sky, I figured it was a matter of time before the rain started.

With the cooler temps and visitors packing up and leaving town, traffic on foot and vehicle was sparse to start the week.

Half of it was white and blue City of Myrtle Beach pickups lumbering about on missions to restore and upkeep the beauty of the beaches and roads.

A guy who looked like he could be Jimmy Buffett's brother cruised past me on a bicycle.

"Mornin'," he said as he passed.

"Morning to you too," I said to his receding back.

I see him often on his bike. He probably lived in a condo down the street. Where was he last Tuesday morning? Did he see someone toting a bulky rug up Flagg Street? Surely, he would have come forward if he did. Everyone who lived here knew about the death of Paige.

That started me down the path I had tried to keep my mind from wandering to. I loved solving problems and puzzles. This would haunt me for a long time. Others might forget, but it would stick with me. Unless someone confessed, or Gomez, or heck, even Moody, figured it out.

A few minutes later, I was speaking to Marilyn. She had an uneventful weekend. Stayed in watching all the movies from the Marvel Cinematic Universe for the fiftieth time. The offseason gave her time to catch up on movie watching.

She asked about Paige.

"I stuck my nose in," I said, "and got it properly whacked for doing so."

"Oh, really?" she said. "What happened?"

I explained the big theatrical scene I arranged and how it all blew up in my face. "Afterwards, Gomez told me to leave it and forget about it."

"But you can't do that, can you, Clark?"

"You know me. I've tried, but I keep going back to it. Not

actively. Just thinking about it."

"There was something else happening that no one knows about except for the killer. You said that you had oil companies and other coworkers on her level as suspects. Big conspiracy theories. What if it was something small? What if it was a spur-of-the-moment decision?"

"Like someone freaked out and clubbed her over the head?"

"Could be. Nothing pre-planned. Maybe the killer thought he could sneak in that morning to do whatever without anyone knowing."

"Then Paige saw them, and they decided it was worth killing her to cover up whatever it was they were doing."

"Yeah, something like that."

The conversation moved on to what was happening in Superman's world in the comics for a bit before my stomach growled. I told Marilyn that I would see her later and walked back towards the store, stopping in at the 8th Ave Tiki Bar for an early lunch and beer.

They seated me by a window with a view of the ocean and beach volleyball courts. I sipped a Landshark lager and watched the waves and people. The hamburgers smelled divine. Kenny Chesney played over the speakers. How Paige ended up on my doorstep rolled through my thoughts.

If it was not big, strong Chris who carried her over his broad shoulders to the alcove, then how did Paige get there? Had to be a car or truck.

She gets whacked and rolled in the rug. Carried downstairs and thrown into a vehicle. Dropped at my place. But why there? If the murderer concealed her in a trunk or truck bed, why not take her to a vacant lot way up in Loris or drive down to

Georgetown and deposit her? Or head inland. Why dump her at Myrtle Beach Reads? Something to do with me?

I pulled out my phone and went back to the notes I took last week. The bits of information on the list did not fit together at the time. Blacked out cameras. The system showed no one using keycards to gain access to the upper level. There was no one shown near Paige's office around the time of her death. The only people with upstairs access was the other executives.

There was the residue on the bottom of the rug. If I could, I would ask Gomez about that. I don't think that came up.

Who did that leave? Chris was out. Mr. John was not capable of pulling something like that off. Two women were at the executive table when I took the coffee there. Linda and Tanzee, I think. They could have worked together to commit the crime, or have help from a significant other, but they seemed as shell-shocked as anyone by Paige's death. There was Martin, the VP. He was older and always boasted about his grandkids. I wasn't sure he could have pulled it off physically even if he hadn't been dropping off the grandkids at daycare.

As I pondered the lack of evidence, a thought struck me. Marilyn suggested that there had to be something else going on around OceanScapes. Perhaps it didn't concern Paige at all.

A few puzzle pieces fell into place. Possibly.

As the server set my burger and fries before me, I made a phone call.

The reporter from WMHF, Erica Sullivan, picked up on the second ring. "Hey, I was thinking about calling you."

"Well, here I am. Quick question. Do you know of anything else going on around the Boardwalk?"

"This time of year, there's not much, but I have one thing."

"What's that?"

"There's this dive bar called The Rogue Storm Cloud."

"I'm familiar with it. Never been in it, though." I could see that restaurant from where I sat on the other side of the volleyball courts.

"They started running poker tournaments out of a backroom, and the police are investigating."

The hair on the back of my neck stood on end. "And card games like organized poker are illegal here?"

"That's right. The only way you can play in a tourney like that is aboard one of the casino ships that cruise out to International Waters."

"Are these tournaments on specific days? How does a person get a seat at the table?"

"Through whispered word-of-mouth, I guess."

"Hmm. Thanks."

The burger and fries were delicious, as usual, and I ordered a second Landshark while the puzzle swirled through the ether, conglomerating into an out-of-focus picture.

Two stops could turn the fuzzy picture into a high-definition blockbuster.

Ominous gray clouds piled up on each other in the distance. A whiff of ozone clung to the air. A storm was coming in more ways than one. As the tide turned on the shore, so it did here.

CHAPTER
THIRTY

The line of storms that formed over Myrtle Beach during my walk up and down the Boardwalk culminated in nothing but a few sprinkles and gusty breezes. That afternoon, I made the two stops, placed a few phone calls, and learned what I suspected was the truth.

I met up with Gomez and Moody and had dinner at the Barbecue House in Surfside, where we hashed out everything. She hadn't been dressed for work and she'd let her hair down, softening her features. As we discussed what went down on the morning of Paige's death, I wondered why Gomez did not have a ring on her finger. She was a catch.

Moody sat on the other side of the table from Gomez and I, grunting and snarling his way through a BBQ platter. At one point, he burped, sat up straight, placed his hands on the table, and said, "I've been doing police work going on thirty years now. Started out on foot and worked my way up the ladder. I've seen it all, but never anything like this." He pointed a barbecue sauce-covered finger at the two of us. "Clark, I barely know you, but I'll say this about you and Gina here. You're two of the smartest people I've come across. I know I don't say much, but that's because I'm watching, and learning. Even at my age, I'm always learning."

Gomez stirred beside me. My cheeks were warm.

Moody continued, "But I figured something out about the case that I'm surprised you two didn't."

"What's that?" Gomez said.

"The residue on the underside of the rug. I know where it came from…"

* * *

The next day, they assembled the same cast of characters from my botched summation plus several others. All the executives, pool staff, and cleaning crew were here, as was Paige's husband. He couldn't break away from his kids the during the first summation attempt. He was the first person Gomez called.

This time, we weren't in a cramped office, but in the basement garage of OceanScapes. The floor, walls, and ceiling were all made of concrete. It was an open area with huge concrete pillars holding up the building above us. The level with the lobby and lower level offices and break rooms sat up on a slope, giving OceanScapes the ability to add this utility area underneath. It smelled like motor oil and cleaning supplies.

A bank of industrial washers and dryers lined one wall. Rolling laundry bins sat to one side that could be wheeled back and forth, transferring sheets and towels from one unit to the other. One washing machine and two dryers hummed with activity.

A ramp led up to the surface from a garage. Various vehicles were parked there. A white pickup truck with a large toolbox behind the cab and three golf carts. Opposite the wall with the laundry facilities was a series of shelves that held folded linens, room supplies like rolls of toilet paper, paper towels, boxes of complimentary toiletries for the bathrooms, and tissue boxes. Three closets surrounded the elevator doors on the third wall. One for electrical, one for maintenance. The third one was unmarked.

Theresa from I Heart Myrtle Beach Tees and Kyle the homeless veteran was here as well. I'll explain their presence later. Sabrina was here against her will. Officers Nichols and O'Brien were present to keep the peace. The larger crowd should have given me bigger jitters than I had the first time I attempted this, but after going over it with Gomez, I had nothing to fear. If I didn't stumble over my words. Which I do occasionally.

"Why are we doing this again?" Mr. John asked with his arms crossed. "Clark already screwed this up once. I don't have time to sit here so this buffoon can attempt to save face."

"Sir," Gomez said, "Clark came to me beforehand this time and laid it out. The only way this was going to happen was if I verified the information first. He's got it this time."

Mr. John relented. "Okay then. Carry on."

"Clark," Gomez said, gesturing to the gathered masses, "the floor is yours."

I took a deep breath. Here goes.

"As you may know," I said, "the issue this case has had has been a lack of evidence. Whoever killed Paige covered their tracks very well. However, I don't think that was their intention. At first, at least."

"You say 'their' like there is more than one person involved," Chris said.

"Correct," I said, "but don't worry. I know it wasn't you and Sabrina working together if that's what you're thinking."

He and Sabrina shared a look. "Okay, get on with it."

I paced back and forth in front of everyone. The motion calmed my nerves.

"I became involved in this at first because Natasha asked me to help because she couldn't trust the police. I dug. I asked questions and put pieces together that didn't necessarily fit. As several of you know, I came up with a theory that wasn't true. And Chris, I'm sorry for implicating you in Paige's death."

He slapped a hand through the air. "No worries, laddie. All water under the bridge."

"Thank you," I said and moved on. "After that, Gomez here told me to forget about it. And I tried hard to do so. The weekend came and went, and I kept myself busy and put the whole mess out of my mind. Then I began thinking about it after a chat with another business owner up on the Boardwalk. The focus had been on who had reason to kill Paige. What was the motive? Then it hit me: what if there was no motive?"

Her husband, Wes, had been quiet, content to listen and stay in the background. Until now. "You mean someone decided to kill her at random?"

"No, not at all. I think they killed her to cover up something else going on here. Well, not here, but on the Boardwalk."

"I'm not following you," Mr. John said.

Gomez stepped in. "Trust me, he's getting to the point."

"Thank you," I said. "Let's narrow this down. One person in this room killed Paige."

That brought a collective gasp from half of those gathered. Unease filled the room. They cast sidelong glances at each other.

Some people created extra space between them and their neighbors. Everyone was now a suspect to the uninformed.

"Who has access to the upstairs offices?" I asked. Most everyone else here knew the answer, but I wanted to get this information in play.

"Only us who have keycards that grant access," Mr. John said. "The other executives and myself."

I raised a finger. "No, there's more than that."

"Then who?"

I leveled the finger at one knot of people. The cleaning crew. They all jumped or jerked at the same time. Julieta's eyes bulged. They shared hurried glances. They separated from each other even further.

"Them," I said. "When I first came here, I spoke to a few of them. James, didn't you tell me you all operate like you're invisible? Like no one notices you're here?"

He cleared his throat. "That's correct, sir."

"Yeah, they have access," Chris said, "but the system showed no keycards were used around that time. We and them can get in because our keycards are coded to open those doors. No one can gain access without them."

"Then why are there keyholes on the doorknobs?"

Blank stares passed between the executives. Except for Martin.

"Yes, when we had the keycard system put in over a decade ago, we integrated the readers in with our current door hardware. We didn't know if we could trust the new readers to always work. They assured us they would, but you never know So we kept the old keys as backups."

"Thanks, Martin," I said. "And who has keys?"

"We do. Us executives," Martin said. "We also keep one at the front desk."

"Anyone else?"

"They do," he said, pointing at the cleaning crew. "There are three that they share."

The corners of my mouth curved down. "Interesting. Now, tell me Martin, Chris, Tanzee, Linda, Mr. John, do you all use the keys you have?"

"No," Mr. John said.

"I don't," Linda drawled. "I don't even keep mine on me. It's in a safe at home."

The other executives murmured similar feelings about the keys.

"Tell me, Detective Gomez, do you have alibis on all the executives?"

"We do. Firm alibis on all of them."

"That narrows it down, doesn't it?" I said, raising my eyebrows to the assembly. "Let's put a pin in that and talk about another nagging detail. The killer made a mistake. If it were me, I would have left her in her office. I had covered my tracks already. Why not let the police believe it was one of you?" I pointed at the executives. "Why not leave her there, wipe my hands of it, sit back, and watch chaos among the bigwigs ensue?

"I'll tell you why. The murder was unplanned. She was killed in the heat of the moment. The murderer had no clue what to do next. So, he hatched a plan. First, roll her up in the rug to limit any bleeding coming from her head. Second, go next door to Chris' office to plant the murder weapon and spray paint. All is fine until this point. Then the murderer made his first mistake. He moved the body out of the offices. Here is where Gomez ran into a dead end. No person or camera saw any people, cars, or trucks near my store after the time of the murder. That leaves the question: How did the rug get to my store?"

"Great question," Mr. John said. "I assume you know the answer."

"I do," I said. "That is why we are here. Two people saw the vehicle carrying the body."

"Who was that?"

"Theresa and Kyle did." I waved a hand at them. Theresa gasped and then hacked and coughed. Kyle gave a toothy grin.

"What? Me? What do you mean?" Theresa said.

"That morning, I walked past Theresa on my way to the end of the building where my store is. Later, I asked her if she had seen any cars or trucks pass by just before I did. She hadn't, but she saw something else." I pointed to the vehicles parked by the garage door. "Tell everyone what you saw."

"Uh," Theresa stammered. "Golf carts. Two of them."

"So, someone stuck her in a golf cart and drove her up the street? How would they do that with her wrapped in a rug?" Chris said. "That would be an incredibly awkward arrangement. Not to mention that it would stick out like a sore thumb."

"Yes, Chris," I said. "It would have been awkward if Paige were actually in the golf cart."

"I don't follow you, son," Mr. John said.

"Let me back up for a second. Yesterday, I went to Julieta's house to ask her a few questions about how their workflow ran. Specifically, the trash. You see, I believe the killer knew when he planted the spray paint can in the trashcan in Chris' office that is left unchecked, it would eventually get taken down here. To the basement."

"So, the killer would have been covered either way," Martin said. "If someone found the spray paint in his trash can, that would implicate Chris in the murder, but if the trash got taken out, then the paint would disappear."

"Exactly. Julieta?"

She jolted. "Si?"

"After you all bring the trash here, what happens?"

"The garbage gets placed in a bin and then taken to a dumpster at the far end of the rear parking lot."

"And how is it transferred there?"

"In a trailer attached to one of the golf carts."

"Goodness," Tanzee whispered to Linda loud enough for everyone to hear.

"Tell me, Detective Moody," I said, "wasn't there some residue on the outward-facing part of the rug?"

"Yes, Clark," he answered with a crooked smile. "There was. Residue waste from trash. The type found in dumpsters."

"How about in trailers dedicated to hauling garbage?"

"Yes," Moody said. "Very possible."

"Thank you," I said and turned to Julieta. "Who was in charge of the trash getting disposed of on your team on the morning of Paige's death?"

She looked behind. Opened her mouth. Closed it. Then blurted, "James was."

I let the full import of that sink in.

"When I first met James," I said, "he told me he was normally off on Mondays and Tuesdays. If so, what was he doing at OceanScapes on the Tuesday of Paige's death? Julieta told me that James switched days off with another member of the maintenance staff at the last minute."

Someone said, "Oh, no."

I held up a finger. "I'll play devil's advocate here. The switch could have just been a coincidence. Or was it? Now we get to my friends Theresa and Kyle here."

Theresa stood at attention when she heard her name again. Her left arm was folded across her chest. The hand clutched her upper arm. She held her right arm down to her side. The ring and middle fingers on that hand were extended, as though clutching an imaginary cigarette. As much as she smoked, it was probably muscle memory. Or a comfort gesture.

Kyle leaned to one side like he was about to fall asleep on his feet, but still held the smile.

They had to be nervous in this position. Most people would be in their shoes.

"Theresa, you said you saw two golf carts that morning. Is one of them in this room?"

"It is."

"Which one is it?"

She pointed a crooked finger at the carts parked behind those facing Gomez and me.

"The one on the left."

Everyone turned. Two carts had normal configurations and were painted a bright blue with the OceanScapes logo placed on the front and sides. The third was identical in coloring, but not in configuration.

It had a dank, black, high-sided metal trailer attached to the rear.

More gasps and hands put to mouths. "That's it," someone said.

"Kyle saw it too. He was sitting under a tree on the other side of the grassy lot behind the store waiting for Veteran's Coffee Hour. He can corroborate the story." Everyone's attention came back to me. "Theresa, who did you see driving it?"

"Him," she bit out between clinched teeth and shifted her finger.

James the janitor was its target.

CHAPTER
THIRTY-ONE

"Wait a minute. Wait a minute," James said, backpedaling. "There's been a big misunderstanding here. It wasn't me."

Neither Gomez nor Officers Nichols and O'Brien jumped to arrest James. There was more work to be done.

"Misunderstanding?" I said. "We'll see. Julieta told me you enjoyed playing cards. Poker, right?"

He was the mouse. I was the cat who had him trapped in a corner.

"From time to time." He waggled his hand.

"That's not what I heard. Don't you go to Julieta's to play cards with her husband and brothers?"

"Naw. Once or twice is all, boss. I'm not that good."

"That's not what I heard," I said. "Julieta?"

"They play every two weeks. He's been to my place twice this month already."

"Does your husband or brothers talk about their card games?"

"Si, senor. They do. They used to play for a lot of money. James cleaned them out every time. Then they switched and started playing with coins instead of cash. He kept coming back, I think, to practice."

"Practice for what?"

"Tournaments."

"Hmm," I grunted for show. "Gomez, I have another question for you. Something that Erica Sullivan from WMHF brought to my attention. Is your department investigating illegal activity happening on the Boardwalk?"

"Why yes, yes we are, Clark," she said. "One bar, The Rogue Storm Cloud, is believed to have been holding illegal, private high-stakes poker matches in a backroom to generate extra income during the offseason. They started recently, but we're trying to determine their origin."

"What has your investigation turned up?"

"We had an anonymous tip from a bitter tourist from up north that this was happening. We suspect that he was involved in at least one of these matches and lost all his money. He said these games occur mid-afternoon during the week. We almost have enough information to get a search warrant. We should have that info soon and shut it down."

"Tell me, Detective Gomez, are details of an investigation such as this something you would divulge to civilians such as us?"

"Not usually, but I feel that we're about to learn more."

"Correct."

James stirred as one Officer approached and stood next to him. The other sidled up beside Paige's husband.

"The day after Paige's death, I was taking a walk up the Boardwalk to my friend's comic book store when I saw James here outside of The Rogue Storm Cloud. I noted the time because I thought it was an odd part of the day. It was just past two thirty. I thought maybe he had gotten off work early as I recalled him saying that he generally got off work around three. Isn't that right, James?"

There was panic in his eyes, but he still answered the question. "That's right, boss."

"You were wearing the same work uniform you're wearing now. Unless you wear that on your off days, you should have been working, right?"

"Aww, I get off a little earlier on Thursdays," he said.

"But this wasn't Thursday, James. It was Wednesday."

He started to speak but thought better of it at this point.

I took my focus off him and addressed everyone else.

"Let me tell you how it went down. Paige arrived at OceanScapes at eight thirty on the dot every other Tuesday to make sure that the payroll got done on time. This time, Paige arrived early because she was going on vacation with her family later that day. When Julieta entered Paige's office, she found it in disarray, with papers scattered everywhere. Sabrina?"

Everyone turned to look at the ex-OceanScapes employee. Gomez forced her to be present. Chris helped get her here.

"Yes, Clark?" she said.

"After Paige's death, weren't you the one in charge of finishing the payroll?"

"I was."

"What were those papers that were dispersed around Paige's office?"

"The time cards."

"Did you find all of them?"

"I didn't."

"How many were missing?"

"One."

"Whose was that?"

It was her turn to point. "James."

Everyone's gaze followed her finger gun back to James. He looked like a caged animal ready to escape. Big Officer O'Brien rested a hand on James' arm as a precaution.

"James was having his buddy Terry here," I pointed to the pool boss, "clock him out on the days James was going to The Rogue Storm Cloud for his poker matches. Then something caused James to get scared that Paige would figure out their scheme. Since he had keys, he had access to every room, including security. He'd seen all the video feeds when he took out the trash in the security room. He knew where the holes were."

I paced back and forth in front of the audience. "He figured he could use a little spray paint on the cameras, sneak in, sneak out and no one would know or suspect it was him. It was early enough that you all didn't have anyone monitoring the feeds, right?"

Martin raised a hand to shoulder level. "Correct. We have two security people. They come in the afternoon before check-in time. Since we record everything, we know we can go back and watch the feeds if something happens. Which it almost never does here."

"Tell me," I said. "Are there any cameras trained on the vehicle pool?"

Everyone looked at the walls above and around where the golf carts and truck were parked. There were no visible cameras.

"There are not," Martin said, confirming what everyone figured out for themselves.

"What about outside the garage door? Any there?"

"Never saw the need. We lock everything up tight, and we keep nothing outside worth stealing."

"Thanks, Martin," I said. "So, James makes his way up to the top of the stairs. Paige's office would have been the first door he passed from his entry point. His goal was the time clocks across from the elevators, but he didn't make it there. Paige was already there. She wasn't expecting anyone. James entered, panicked, and killed her. He wrapped the body, came down the stairs, and around the back of the building. He opened the garage door, tossed Paige in the trash trailer, and took off up the street. Everything was going fine until he saw Theresa throwing boxes away behind her shop. He freaked out even more, stopped, ditched the body, and kept going."

Heads nodded. People whispered to each other, cautious of making direct eye contact with James. He stared at a hole in the floor in front of his feet.

"Am I close to what happened, James?"

He grunted and kicked an invisible rock.

"What's that?" I said.

He blinked so hard that the lines on his forehead looked like canyons.

"I have to give you credit," he said. "You nailed it."

A monumental weight lifted from my shoulders. If the situation hadn't been so grim, I would have smiled.

"I thought about it the night before," he said. "That Paige was a sharp woman. She'd wonder why Terry and I were clocking out at the same time. We got away with it the first week. But I know her. She'd see the pattern. She was here earlier than usual, and I didn't know what to do."

"That didn't end up happening," I said. "She was in the

middle of inputting the times into her system when you entered her office."

"Yup. I panicked. I came in to remove my card before she could process them. I hit her. She stopped breathing and I couldn't feel a pulse anymore. I freaked out, man."

At his confession, O'Brien tightened his grip on James' arm. Nichols rested a hand on Mark's shoulder. He began to cry.

"But why? Why go to that extreme of covering it up?" Mark choked. "She was a mom to four wonderful kids and my wife of twenty-three years. Now she's gone. Forever. Why man, why?"

"It was the money," James confessed. "Pure and simple. I got word that The Rogue Storm Cloud was going to do these poker games in their backroom. I had to pay a thousand dollars to get a seat at the table. Terry helped front the money the first time for me splitting the winnings with him. He'd clock me out when I played."

"But you two didn't clock out at the same time, did you?"

"No. That was the glitch in our system."

"He clocks out at three-thirty and I clock out at four," Terry said, not wanting to let his friend go down in flames by himself. "But I couldn't leave my post across the street when he was supposed to get off, clock him out, come back, wait a few minutes, and then go clock myself out for the day. I couldn't. I have too much to do when wrapping up my day. I figured I'd clock us out at the same time and go home. It would look like he was working a little over. OceanScapes doesn't pay him directly anyway."

"We, I mean, they don't," Sabrina said. "Paige puts the cleaning crew's hours in a separate report and shoots it off to their outsourcing company. They let us know if the cleaning crew was working too much overtime."

"I didn't know that," James said, squeezing his eyes shut, hopefully realizing that he didn't need to kill Paige after all. "I bet I know the snitch at the poker games you're referring to, Detective. He was some pasty Yank from New York who thought he was the king of poker and wanted to throw his money around."

"How much money did you win in these games, James?" Gomez asked.

"Twenty, thirty thousand dollars. Somewhere in there."

"Holy cow," Chris said. "I'm in the wrong profession."

James looked at him. "I know you, man. You don't have what it takes to be a poker player, like me."

"The only place you're going to be playing poker is in prison, bub," I said. "You may be a superb poker player, but you're a lousy murderer."

O'Brien placed James' hands behind his back.

Gomez stepped up to him. "James, you're under arrest for the murder of Paige Whitaker. Anything you say may be used against you in a court of law…"

She finished reading him his rights. I looked at the ceiling and let out a breath, thinking about Autumn.

This was for her.

CHAPTER
THIRTY-TWO

A few minutes later, O'Brien and Nichols led James and Terry out a side entrance in handcuffs.

The OceanScapes staff milled about, talking amongst themselves. Mr. John, Chris, and the other executives came up and thanked me. Paige's husband gave me a bear hug. Moody smiled at me. It was jarring.

Gomez asked me and a few others to come with her to the police station and give statements.

It was a long afternoon and evening.

* * *

After the sun had gone down and most of the OceanScapes people left, Gomez and I stood outside of the police department. A light breeze ruffled the palm trees. Crickets chirped. Streetlights crackled in random patterns.

I looked out at the parking lot and watched Natasha drive away. She told me while we were waiting in the police station that she hadn't lost her job. To the contrary, they promoted her to Sabrina's cash office position.

The events from the past week rushed back to me in a

kaleidoscope of images. Finding the dead body, pinning the murder on Chris, screwing that up, and eventually solving the mystery. It was a surreal position I never saw myself being in.

Gomez patted me on the back. "Great job, Clark. I've never seen anything like it outside of TV and books. A civilian solving a murder."

"Thanks," I said. "I felt like I had to do something."

"And that's an admirable quality, Clark. You were focused on so few people that you didn't see any other leads. At first. Then you saw, learned, and remembered things we hadn't. The mayor will doubtless give you a commendation for this, you know."

"I don't want any awards."

"Ah, don't worry about it. You'll get it at an informal ceremony in his office. Might be a reporter with a camera, but that's it."

"We'll see."

"Remember," she said. "Means, motive, opportunity."

I smiled. "Yeah, I realize that now."

"Bear that in mind next time."

I turned to look at her. "Next time?"

A corner of her mouth turned upward in a smile. She cocked her head to one side. "You know, in case I ever get stuck on a case, I might call you and pick your brain."

"I don't know," I laughed. "We'll see about that."

"Keep an open mind. I know you will." She grinned. "I mean, how else could you have put this together?"

"Okay." I wasn't sure helping in a police investigation was something I wanted to do again, but I let life take it where it wants me. Push the envelope. Watch it bend.

"Good." She placed a hand on mine. Not flirty. More of a sympathetic touch.

"You know," Gomez said, "I liked your wife. She was a kind woman and good at her job. I wasn't part of that investigation. I didn't get promoted to my position until recently. After her death, I wondered if she was too good. Know what I mean?"

My ears flushed. "No, I don't know what you mean."

"Part of me wondered if her death wasn't solely by natural causes."

My heart pounded. I stammered, "What?"

She looked me square in the face. "I think she was murdered."

To Be Continued...

ACKNOWLEDGMENTS

I would like thank Dr. Stephanie Rose for lending me her advice on murdery subjects. My thanks go to Taylor Hernandez for helping to lend some realism for the reporter scenes. Thanks to Haley Mellert, Angie Barnhardt, Terri Barley, CariAnn Sparks, and my mom for volunteering to read an early draft of this novel and providing feedback.

All mistakes are mine.

I'll see you on the Boardwalk!

ABOUT THE AUTHOR

Caleb is a member of the International Thriller Writers and Southeastern Writers Association, the author of five novels, social media marketer, woodworker, occasional golfer, reacher of things on high shelves, beach walker, shark tooth finder, and munchkin wrangler.

His two Lucas Caine Adventure novels, *Blackbeard's Lost Treasure* and *The Search for the Fountain of Youth*, were both Semi-Finalists for the Clive Cussler Adventure Awards Competition.

He is currently at work on the next book in the Myrtle Beach Mystery Series.

He lives in Myrtle Beach with his wife and son (the munchkin).

Visit Caleb online at

www.CalebWygal.com

If you enjoyed this story please
consider reviewing it online and at Goodreads,
and recommending it to family and friends.